T H E
&
Y

Other Stories

In memory of
KIM CLERC (1947-1996)
and
ARLEN J. HANSEN (1936-1993)

The Y

and
Other
Stories

by

Charles Clerc

Provine Press
Berkeley, California
1997

Portions of this work have previously appeared, in slightly
different form, in the following publications: *Best Articles
and Stories, Daedalus, Facet, Pacific Review, San Jose Studies,
Satire Newsletter, War, Literature, & the Arts, Western Humanities
Review.*

Library of Congress Catalog Card Number: 96-071248
ISBN: 1-889883-01-8

Provine Press
1941 Delaware Street
Berkeley, California 94709

Printed in the United States of America, 1997

About the Author

CHARLES CLERC (pronounced *Clair*) turned to full-time writing upon retirement from a distinguished teaching career. After earning his Ph.D. at the University of Iowa, he became Professor of English and department chairman at the University of the Pacific, in Stockton, California, where he taught for thirty years. Besides earlier teaching at the universities of Utah and Iowa, he also later served as a visiting professor at the Air Force Academy and the University of Bern, Switzerland.

Clerc's previous books include *Approaches to "Gravity's Rainbow,"* *Stockton: Heart of the Valley—A Contemporary Portrait*, and three editions of the popular anthology *Seven Contemporary Short Novels*. In addition to the fifteen stories in this collection, some half of which have been published, he has produced a play, *The Pillar*. Also, his numerous essays have appeared in such magazines and journals as *Newsweek*, *Journal of Modern Literature*, *Studies in Short Fiction*, *Midwest Quarterly*, *Modern Fiction Studies*, and *English Journal*.

An Idahoan by birth, a war veteran, and father of a son and three daughters, Clerc writes and travels in western Europe, for the most part in Switzerland, and in the States from his home base in California. He is presently at work on a novel and a memoir.

This book of stories is dedicated
to classmates and our teachers,
to colleagues, and, with special
gratitude, to my own students, all
of whom made the experience of
living throughout its time period
from 1938 to 1997 memorable.

It's also for
Claudette,
Caroline,
Rebecca.

CONTENTS

INTRODUCTION

TELL ME A STORY

By Donald Anderson

Welcome to *The Y and Other Stories*, a collection in which
Charles Clerc's characters are as likely to trade in isolation,
madness, death, or bitterness as they are to trade in
optimism, faith, life, and humanity. Indeed, it is this
disorderly and full range that makes this collection so
worthy. Clerc is a brave writer who stretches his voice and
does not seek after music of one style or octave. Another
attraction of Clerc's collection is the span—the sixty years
that the stories cover. They are arranged so that the first
story, "Friday Night at Pineapple's," is set in late 1938,
with the last, "J'accuse," ending in 1997. At least one of
the collection's fifteen stories takes place in each of seven
separate decades.

"The Y" as title for this collection works especially
well, offering, as it does, connotations of juncture, deci-
sion-making, alternate routes. The "Y" in the title story—
the confluence of two unnamed rivers—presents a physical

i

location for a clear-cut dilemma: two brothers negotiating over the future of a completed affair and a pregnant woman. In fact, all the stories, like examined lives, involve choices: what to do? which direction to go? what is wrong or perfectly right? As I've suggested, Clerc's characters are more often than not caught between opposites: fullness and emptiness, meaning and vacuity, humanity and nihilism, comedy and tragedy, maturity and fecklessness, reality and artificiality, and on and on. Thematic subjects range far and wide as well: initiation, love, falseness, generativity, alienation, discord, superficiality, integrity, decency, goodness, friendship.

To my taste, the two best stories are "The War" and "LOCKE-HAVEN AT LARGE." In "The War," we witness a deadly duel between a boy and an old man that is best read at an allegorical level—the brinkmanship, say, of the United States and the Soviet Union during the perilous cold war, though, as our daily news will daily remind us, escalated violence *is* escalated violence. In the tradition of Huck Finn and Holden Caulfield, Truman "Chip" Mackie witnesses a hard world in "LOCKE-HAVEN AT LARGE," then faithfully and naïvely reports it. We see, too, the consequences of war in a world poised on a fulcrum, all events in the story occurring in the exact middle of the twentieth century.

Though arranged chronologically, the stories can be read in any order, and there is something for everyone: bull-fighting; a comedy of errors aboard a Liberty ship in Canadian waters; the surreal bifurcated life of an actor; duplicitous lives told by photographic slides in a San Francisco penthouse; the brambles of academe prickling in two separate stories; a humorous vignette of adultery and crime spun out in a casino on the Strip; a narcissistic author promoting her sexploitation book on tour; football, puppy love, and lunacy in a shoe-shine parlor; primitive Russian troops sacking an abandoned film studio. It's all Clerc country.

And this: There are those who would say that literature is no longer sacred, if not dead. How can this be? Whose earliest recollection does not include, on some level, the request Tell Me a Story? The human race needs stories. We need all the experience we can get.

Donald Anderson is editor of *War, Literature, and the Arts: An International Journal of the Humanities*, and is a 1996-97 recipient of a Creative Writers' Fellowship Grant from the National Endowment for the Arts. His most recent book is *Aftermath: An Anthology of Post-Vietnam Fiction* (Henry Holt, 1995).

The Y

and
Other
Stories

FRIDAY NIGHT AT PINEAPPLE'S

Autumn dusk is descending as he comes to his after-school job at the shoe shine parlor. Lights from the *Ritz*, the movie theater across the street, begin winking on and off and chasing each other up and down the marquee. The same double bill has been on for a week: *You Can't Take It With You* and *Jezebel*, with Pathe News.

Three of his schoolmates standing near the box office wave and beckon for him to come over. The traffic light at the corner changes and when the line of cars has passed, they are already inside the theater. He straightens his shoulders at the doorway where the odor of shoe polish and dye hangs as heavy as gas. Lights gleam from the linoleum and dazzle in the long mirror along one wall.

His father is talking to himself at the back but stops when he hears footsteps.

"Ah, Herakles. Ain't you early?"

"Yah, because of the game today. It's not like practice nights, remember?"

"Yah yah." His father winces. "What's that?"

"Just a bruise."

"You got hurt. You okay?"

"Sure."

"What's all that red stuff?"

"Merthiolate."

"What you say?"

"Merthiolate. Like iodine."

At the mirror he pushes his tongue against his cheek and squints. "It's nothing, just a strawberry." The swivel chairs on the platform are lined up in the mirror like a backfield posing for a picture.

His father points in the direction of an old radio in the corner of a display cabinet. "I listened the game, part of it. The man on the radio he talks so fast I can't understand. I had a customer, Mr. Packer, from the bank, with the Cordovans and the build-up heels, he was listening. He says, hey, ain't that your boy they're talking about? Can you beat that? They said, Herk Panopolis, he done this and he done that. Why they call you this funny name? Anyways, I was plenty surprise, believe you me. You did good, Herakles, real good."

"Thanks, Pop."

"You boys sure did skonk them."

"We got a good team."

His father strokes the rounded top of the radio. "You bet, the whole town listens every game. Mr. Packer, he said this team she makes state champs again."

He nods. "We got a chance."

"Mr. Packer he explains me what you done. This player you knock over, he's okay? I don't know, this football, she's pretty rough."

"He's okay. He didn't play in the game anymore, though." He leans against the display cabinet, fingering the keys of the cash register. It is nickel plated, with fancy scrolling along the top, and red, white, and blue keys. Only the white keys on one side are worn. He looks, unseeing, into the street. "It's kind of funny. I made just one good tackle. I didn't do anything else any good. It's like I was a big hero or something."

"But you was, son, that's what Mr. Packer says, and the man on the radio: you was all by yourself, you did a perfect something, that you smashed up the boy with the ball to keep him from going over the goal post. The man on the radio, he says you was a pretty tough little monkey, something about getting run into by a truck, you know, a Max truck."

He grins, then shakes his head. "Yah, I guess we would have been scored on, the first time in six games. But I still can't figure it out. We were ahead 33 to 0 when it happened."

A customer comes into the parlor.

"I'll get him, Pop."

His father starts toward the customer's chair with a sidling motion that in its immediacy and fluidity is hardly motion at all. "No, that's okay, son. You get your apron. No rush. Sit down and rest up."

"Make it a quick one, Sam," the customer says.

"Yes sir, Mr. Simpson, right away, you bet."

The customer pulls a half-folded newspaper from under his arm and glances at the headlines. "Way them Krauts are pushing their weight around over there in Europe, don't look good, Sam."

"No sir, she's looking bad, real bad." His father's brow furrows darkly.

"And that Mussolini joker, he ain't exactly sitting still neither."

At the back of the shop that is partitioned from the platform by a curtain, he hangs up his jacket, and rolls up his sleeves. He selects a clean white apron from a shelf. The two men are still conversing in the front but the subjects change from the menace of Hitler's Nazis to a current ad for Simpson's Used Trucks, then to the football game played that afternoon at the high school stadium. In a cabinet he finds a bottle of brilliantine hair oil and rubs some into his shower-dry hair. He picks out an apple from three in a small wicker basket his father made once and munches on it.

The game is in his mind again, flipping in pictures like the film strips he saw the day before in his biology class. The action has feel too: the parched cottonish sand in his mouth when the coach sent him in—as first scrub—to play, the bounce of his half-size-too-large helmet, the woolen itchiness of his scrubteam jersey, out of place beside the satiny finish of the varsity uniforms. He blocked and tackled and carried the ball twice but all that was blurry, except for one moment when he rolled over from underneath a pile and looked into the lowering sun. And then came the sequence leading up to the tackle, in slow motion and in such clarity that he seemed to be looking at it through a magnifying glass. He could see the play developing at the scrimmage line from way back in his safety position. Everybody had expected the Lions to kick on fourth down, including himself. But they hadn't and Ty Nemo was out in the clear, running at him hard along the sideline, with his knees high but up straight, a fancy dan, carrying the ball with one hand like a loaf of bread, the way the coach in the skull sessions said he would run, their big gun, all-league, a senior, just Nemo and himself, as if the other players disappeared, the referees, the grandstands, the field, everything. He saw it again before he dove, the confident mean grin on Nemo's face. Then the picture had feel again: the *thwack* of shoulder pads against knees, the *roomph*ing grunt, the twist, the skidding roll across the grass, the ball squirting out of bounds. Then he felt himself standing up with his hands on his hip pads, the pain in his cheek, breathing hard, spitting out chalk line dust, and

4   *Friday Night at Pineapple's*

looking down at Nemo. The screen blurred after the cluster formed around Nemo and carried him off the field.

Another customer comes in and he steps out to get him, a wingtip two-tone. During a flurry of business he and his father work silently. In the lull that follows, he straightens out the magazines in the magazine rack, all new issues of *Collier's*, *The Saturday Evening Post*, *Bluebook*, *Life*, *Liberty*, and a dozen more, provided by his mother from the hotel where she is a chambermaid. Then he sweeps the floor and washes down the sidewalk. He also wipes down the sign at the curb that reads SHOES SHINED in black letters above a red arrow. Its identical sides are lit up by neon from the drug store on the left, the jewelry store on the right. His father comes out to smell the clean wet cement and then returns to the back of the shop.

He is sitting on the bench near the big window in front watching traffic go by when Diana comes in. His cheek-bones turn hot. He stands up. His arms and legs feel prickly.

Her red lipstick glistens. "Hello, Harry," she says. Her tongue flicks across her lower lip. "I want a shoe shine."

He looks at the floor and out at the street. His father is still in the back. He motions with his head to the platform steps.

She is carrying an umbrella. When she places it beside her chair it clatters to the floor. "Oh dear," she says. He takes it to the coat rack by the door and hangs it up beside his father's cap and cane.

The heat remains in his face as he holds her feet by the insteps and tries to position her shoes into the footrests. She holds her knees tightly together so that the soles of her shoes are not down flat.

"Do you think you can make them shine?"

He glances up after studying her shoes. Her feet are so small—he would never have believed them to be that small. "Yah," he says. She's laughing at him, he's sure. He tries to wipe the polish from his hands onto his apron. He's sure that she can see his heart pounding through his shirt.

Her shoes are scuffed but not dirty. They're plain brown with a low heel and will take a good shine. He likes to shine good shoes. Even more, he likes to shine good shoes that are very dirty, as long as they don't have oil or grease on them. He has been working off and on for three nights at a pair of high-top boots on a counter in the back. They were brought in all covered with mud, but now they dazzle when he turns them in the light.

He takes a soapy brush from a pan set in an open shelf under the platform and scrubs her shoes. After wiping them, he fans them with a shine rag. He glances up. She is watching him, her mouth slightly open, the tip of her tongue held between her teeth.

"What are you doing that for?"

"I have to get them dry."

"Oh. Did you get to play in the game today?"

"A little bit."

"Somebody said you did something real neat, but I guess I wasn't looking. What did you do?"

"Not much. I was in only a couple minutes."

"That's not so . . . you—" She stops. He is intent on applying the first coat of polish on her right shoe and doesn't look at her. She laughs. "All those numbers. I can't tell who's who. You might have been Tommy O'Hara for all I know." When he makes no response, she says, "Did you hear the cheer we gave you?"

He straightens and hesitates. "Naw. You can't hear much of anything out on the field."

"Well, it was a loud cheer. Is that where you got your face hurt?"

"Yah."

"I'll bet it hurts."

"Not too much."

"Why don't you put something over it?"

"Coach says it will heal faster this way."

"Oh."

He bends over her shoes again. His mouth is dry and he works it. He rotates his shoulder to get his shirt collar over the back of his neck where a pustule is coming in. She's staring right at his hairline, he's sure. Sweat runs down his back. When he bends close to her, he can smell her perfume over the odor of the polish. He wipes his forehead with the back of his hand. His shirt is plastered to him.

"Aren't you going to the prom tonight?" she asks. Her shoes keep slipping off the footrests as she bends forward and hugs her knees.

"Naw. I got to work."

"I thought maybe you'd asked somebody."

He hunches and says nothing.

"That's too bad. I'm going with Joey."

"Joe Anderson?" he blurts. His face hot, he bends to inspect a tiny nick in her toe.

"Uh huh."

A customer enters and starts to climb into the first chair from the floor level.

"That way, mister." He has never seen him before.

"Yeah." The customer turns back, springs up the platform steps, and spins around in his chair. "Hey, how about that." The customer attacks his chewing gum again, teeth showing.

He turns to call his father, who already approaches from the back. Passing the girl, his father smiles, head tilted toward her.

"Yes sir," his father says, adjusting the customer's shoes into their footrests and stroking the leather.

The customer is adjusting a tie in which bamboo shoots and mint green palm fronds wage war on a cocoa battle-field. "Shine 'em up good, pops, and make it snappy." The customer pats the tie and makes a Popeye chin at himself in the mirror.

"Yes sir, you bet," his father says, dipping the scrub brush into the pinkish lather.

The customer looks up at the big round middle chande-lier above him and then into the mirror at the girl who hugs her knees tighter.

Her feet do not stay in the rests. He positions them again, forcing himself to keep his head down. At least she's not like Miss Dorfmeyer, one of his teachers, who didn't seem to care at all about keeping her skirt down or her legs together. Once she sat down, he never looked up. She always wore big, thick heeled shoes with holes in the top that were hard to shine. One time she came back and complained that he got polish on her stockings.

"Say, pops, this platform's pretty snazzy," the customer says. "Whirly chairs and all. Never saw no shine parlor with this kind of set-up."

"It is my own idea. Ulixes, he is my son in the col-lege—this is my other son—he draws up the plans from my head. The government, she is giving me a patents, yes sir."

"Patent, eh. How about that."

"I have not receive the papers yet, but they come, you bet. If that Roosevelt don't keep poking his nose in my business."

"Yeah, that's FDR for you. What happened to the kid there—you belt him?"

"Belt?" His father's shoulders are drawn up. "My boy is a player of the football."

"What's he play?" The customer sizes him up.

"He plays in the back."

"In the back, huh. What position, kid?"

"Left half," he says, without looking up.

"Maybe you'll get one of them whatchamacallits where they pay you to play college ball. Ride the gravy train. Do nothing but make touchdowns on Saturday. How about that, kid?"

"I don't know, mister," he says from his bent position. "I just started high school."

"Don't you think I can tell that, kid." The customer winks at the girl who in turn smothers a giggle. "Yeah, 'bout the only way they make it is that free ride," the customer adds, turning his head this way and that to the mirror. "Most of these athaletes—nothing between the ears."

"What you mean what you say?" his father says. "Herakles, he makes always the, how you say it, the roll of honor. And he is a vice president too." His father faces the girl. "Ain't that right, miss?"

She colors. "Yes, Harry is vice president of our class."

"Yeah," says the customer, turning to her. "You go to school with him?"

"We're in Spanish together . . . and biology."

"Spanish? You mean the lingo? Hey, that's rich. You and him learning how to talk spic."

He keeps his face down. He knows it is oily. His back and chest feel wrapped in flames, and he holds his arms close to his body to conceal his sweating. His face low over the shoes, he absorbs himself in applying the rest of a second coat of polish. He uses his fingers, as his father insists. No good shiner ever put polish on with a brush or a rag. It's all in the fingers, putting on just the right amount, smoothly, not too heavily, twice over, until the leather squeaks under his hand. He can tell that his father is finishing up the customer in a hurry.

The customer's head is craned around. "What's that flag crossed there with the 'Merican flag?"

"That is the Greek flag, mister," his father says.

"Greek, huh. I asked somebody where to get a shine in this burg, they told me Pineapple's. Now that sure ain't Greek. That's your Hawaii, someplace like that. Pineapple ain't Greek."

"It is Panopolis," his father says. "The correct full name is Demodocus Samouel Panopolis, and this here is Herakles."

"That's a mouthful of Greek all right."

"I am born by village near Alexandroupolis in Thrace, but now I am a naturalize citizen. My sons they are Americans born here, not Greece. So no difference, same like you."

"Says you," the customer replies. "No call to have that flag there, pops. You ain't in no Greece. This is America."

He knows it's coming even before his father makes the sound. He hunches his shoulders against it, but that doesn't stop it from coming: the teeth grinding together. He watches his father's jaw muscles jump and knot. He bends farther down.

"So you come again, you Turk," his father says.

"Wha'd you say?" the customer says.

His shoulders drawn up and hunched, he looks sideways at his father and whispers, "Pop, please." Sweat falls from his face.

His father snaps the shine rag like a cracking whip over the customer's toes, throws it down, and stands back, arms folded. His knobby jaws jump, and his eyelids are held in slits.

"You're all done, mister."

"Wha'd he say?"

"Nothing."

The customer looks at his shoes and nods, "Good enough." Light dazzles at the toes. The customer starts to step down.

"You go that way."

The customer spins in his chair and bounce-steps to the doorway. "What's the damages?"

His father still says nothing and flicks his head at the sign, his jaws working. The customer flips a quarter and says, "Keep the change, pops." His father makes no attempt to catch it, and the coin hits him in the chest. The customer is already out the door. His father strides grim-eyed toward the back and stands facing the last chair.

"I'll get it, Pop." He retrieves the coin, rings up the amount of the shine, and puts a dime in a slot to the side. He returns to finish the girl's shine. With a quick move-ment of her elbow in the direction of the door, she makes a face like the monkey in the zoo at the edge of town when he spits at people. Then she smiles and lowers her eyes. He grins. Her tongue darts out to wet her underlip, and he hears a short breath from her. He is smiling so broadly he nearly laughs.

"Turk, you betcha," his father says to the empty chair. "In cahoots with the police. Give them a inch and they take a mile. You betcha, in cahoots, the whole bunch, the sheriff, he's one of them. The Turks, they come and spy on you, and they torture you. They cut you with knives across up down. What they done to the village. Like animals, animals."

The girl's head turns sharply toward the street.

He stops his brushing and stands straight before her. "So I guess you're going to the dance with Joey, huh. Who else is going? I guess everybody, huh?"

His father stops talking and glowers at the chair.

"Yes," she says in a small voice.

"That's—that's nice." He bends and applies the brush to her shoes. He has to be careful around the upper edges next to the white anklets. He wants to finish her up as fast as possible before his father starts in again about the Turks and the police and the sheriff in cahoots with Roosevelt, but the brush is leaving a mark on the top side of her shoe. He takes a shine rag, and with the smooth side of it held tight over one of the footrests he runs the brush up and down against it.

She watches him and gives a little laugh. "Harry, my foot is over here."

"It's to keep the brushes clean."

"Oh."

He hunches himself to the shine rag, nothing fancy, though, no whips, no snaps. He keeps at it methodically until his face looks as round as a fifty-cent piece in each shoe.

She wiggles her toes. "You're making my foot all—all warm."

His hands are sweaty. When he's applying the sole dye, he drops the toothbrush. He flinches when she giggles. He wipes the soles dry and straightens. "That's it," he says.

Her chin rests on her knees. "They look real nice." She wriggles her toes again. "How much is it, Harry?"

His nose is nearly touching her hair. He looks into the glinty curls and down the slope of her forehead. When he doesn't answer for a second, she looks up, her eyes large on his.

He takes a step backward and casts his eyes downward. "It's fifteen cents."

She unsnaps her coin purse and places a quarter gingerly into his dirty hand. When she starts to step down, he puts his hand on the chair and partially turns it.

"You go that way, down the steps."

"Oh, I forgot."

He rings up 15¢ and takes a dime from the register. He drops it back in and rubs his palms up and down his apron. Then he retrieves it. He places it in her palm with his hand formed as if he's trying to make the shadow of a deer on the wall.

"Thanks," he mutters.

"Thank you, Harry," she says, and carefully places the dime in her purse. She looks down at her shoes and again moves her toes. "Golly, they're just like a mirror."

He makes no reply. He was going to remind her of her umbrella, but she has already taken it down. He toys with the string of his apron and she zips and unzips her purse.

"I have to go," she says. She looks toward the back. "Well, goodbye, Mr. Panopolis."

His father is talking to the empty chairs about the Turks and the police and doesn't respond. He trembles in his anguish, looks at the girl, then away from her into the street.

The girl takes a deep breath and says in a firm voice, "Well, goodbye, Mr. Panopolis."

His father blinks twice. Then his father's face breaks into a sunny smile as he turns and takes a few steps toward the girl. "Same to you, miss, and come in again, you bet."

Her mouth works. "Oh, thank you very much." She steps backward and looks from his father to him. He reaches down for a corner of his apron to wipe the sweat from his face. Her eyes dart. "I didn't know you wore aprons," she says, adding over her shoulder and almost out the doorway, "Bye, Harry."

"Yeah, see you," he says.

He retreats to the back. He scrubs his hands with borax and a small brush until not a speck of polish is left on them.

When he reenters the front, a customer is just leaving. His father is ringing up the sale of a can of polish. He checks the sections where the polish is kept and sees that he'll have to put in some more black. He does not want to look at his father and keeps himself occupied with the polish cans.

His father hooks a finger in his collar and works it back and forth behind the black leather bow tie. "That smart-aleck bastard, he——"

"Forget it, Pop."

"You hear what he says about the flag."

"He was just a big mouth."

His father straightens his bow tie and runs a hand over his coarse gray hair. "You're right, son, that's what he was."

"Do me a favor, please, Pop. Don't talk about the game anymore, will you?"

"Sure." His father's eyes glisten a velvety brown. "Who was that girl that was in here?"

"Just a girl I know from school."

"How is she called?"

"Diana. Diana Calidon."

"Calidon . . . Mr. Calidon, the big cheese man? He comes in here ever once in a while. That is his daughter, eh? Seems a very nice young lady."

"She's all right."

"I hear the girl say something to the effect of a dance."

"Yah, it's tonight at the school."

"We're not going to be very busy tonight, Herakles. Why don't you go?"

"Naw, we'll be busy."

"I can take care for tonight."

"Forget it, Pop. It's too late."

"What you mean?" his father says. "You got plenty time."

"I don't mean that. You wouldn't understand. It's too late to—" His hands almost touch his father's sleeve but go instead to the cash register. He puts his fingers on the keys as if at a typewriter. "Never mind about it."

A customer bounds up the steps, flops himself into the second chair, and whirls around.

"Attaboy, young fella," the customer says. "Shine 'em up good. Say, what dark alley you been in?"

The chairs stay full until nine o'clock. Some of the varsity players come in for shines and kid him about the bruise on his cheek. They smell of shaving lotion and sit with corsage boxes on their laps. Once his father starts in again about the Turks in cahoots with the sheriff and Roosevelt, but the customers are all talking and there's a waiting line too, so nobody pays any attention, and soon his father is smiling again.

At a quarter to ten he sweeps the floor and the platform and cleans up the bins. He brings the sign in from the sidewalk, then pulls down the shade on the door and turns the lights down in the front. As he changes Friday to Saturday on the calendar, he looks at the fancy pictures inside the zodiac above the date. His father has finished dusting. While his father counts the bills, dollars, half-dollars, and quarters, he counts the dimes, nickels, and pennies, rotating his shoulders to try to ease the ache in his back. He turns out the lights. As his father locks up the shop, the marquee lights of the theater across the street go dark.

They walk together to the bicycle rack around the corner. The combination lock on his bicycle is faced away from the street light and it takes him two tries to get it open. He rides a little way ahead of his father. Away from the street lights on the dark sidewalks, the stars bunch brightly, like milk splattered down the sky. Through trees, he can see the glow of lights from the high school gym. It is so quiet that he can hear faint strains of the music.

His father stops, cane hooked over his forearm, and buttons up his sweater to the neck and pulls down his cap bill. "You should be there at this school, Herakles, having yourself a nice time. The boys tonight, they wished for you to be there. This school, they will have another dance, won't they?"

"Sure, I guess so."

"Herakles, you ask that girl that was in tonight to go with you to this next dance. She is sweet on you, anybody can see that."

"Aw, Pop, how do you know?"

"I will get Thoros to come in from Louie's. We buy you a suit of clothes. I will tell Mama. She will holler, you can bet on that, but don't you worry."

"Aw, Pop, you don't know."

"I know, I'm telling you, I hear it in the voice. You ask this young lady to the dance. You take her there and you have yourself a nice time and this is final. I want no talk back."

"If you say so."

"You bet I say so. Now, come on, we go home." His father begins to sing softly, a song about one of the heroes of ancient Greece. "Such a night. Going to be a beautiful day tomorrow. Ain't that right, Herakles, beautiful."

He continues to ride ahead of his father, slow pedaling, stopping to wait, while his father now and then lifts the cane right and left and ahead, as if to ward off enemies of the dark.

IN THE CANNON'S MOUTH

"Son of an ox," Private Boris Platochuk growls. "What does it look like?"

"A clothing market," Private Vasili Senovich Ulkyakhtakuva replies.

"Dumb ox," Private Platochuk spits. "Can you not see these are special clothes. It is where the costumes are kept."

"Ah, for dancing," Private Aleksai Andianovich Nobokof says.

"You were weaned on sour goatmilk," Private Platochuk says.

"These are costumes for the cinema," says Private Yury Mikhail Konstantin. He has just been transferred from another unit that was almost wiped out by short rounds the day before, and he has not yet learned the names or origins of his comrades.

"What is the cinema?" asks Pavel as he pisses against the door. He has no other name, nor has he rank now. Because he struck an officer three days earlier on the outskirts of the city he is to be courtmartialed and shot, if the officer remains alive when the city has been secured. Pavel shakes himself.

"So waves the tail of the bull," says Private Josef Sejonovitsch Smokotin.

"Did you see that cow this morning in the street?" asks Private Konstantin.

"She bled from the mouth like a stream," Private Platochuk says.

"It is an image that I shall retain and use upon return to my study," says Private Konstantin. "Imbedded like silver the shrapnel, and the black and white of her body, and she floated in the wine of her life."

"Wine," Private Ulkyakhtakuva scoffs, "he calls it wine. Blood and dung and flies."

"This is the wine of life," Private Smokotin grins as he takes from his tunic a bottle of rubbing alcohol.

Private Nobokof takes the same kind of bottle from his tunic.

"Did that butcher of a cook get her?" asks Private Platochuk, his bottle to his lips. "Maybe we will have a decent meal for a change. Those horses yesterday. You saw what those pigs did. Sliced down to the bone. There with the flies. The pigs. Nobody eats a horse. Where I am from they hang a man by the tongue who eats a horse."

"You would eat it if you were hungry," says Private Konstantin.

Private Smokotin belches against the fire in his throat. "I have been in those mountains—he knows what he says." He takes his submachine gun from its cradle in his arm and holds it by the small of the stock. "We got that warehouse next door, eh, *brrt, brrrrt.*"

"You should not have fired into the parcels," says Private Konstantin. "It was a place of the Red Cross. Did you not see the medicines running over the floor?"

Private Smokotin is ready to protest, but upon the crash of a barrage his shoulders hunch and his neck collapses inward like a turtle's.

Private Platochuk cocks his ear and raises his head. "Ah, those Katushkas, what a racket."

"Like Murmansk, on the docks where I was raised," Private Konstantin says from where he has ducked against a wall. "When two ships grind together. The steel grinds along my entire backbone."

The sound is gone, and the men begin to move again.

Konstantin sees a bathroom to the side and his face breaks into a smile. "Thanks be to God," he says as he enters and strips to the waist. "Blast, no soap," he frowns. But he washes anyway and the others crowd in, open-mouthed, to watch him. When he finishes they turn the water faucets on and off again and again. They roar as they take turns switching the light on and off.

At the washbowl they splash water over one another. As no one is using the toilet to wash, Pavel washes himself in it. Nobokof sits in the bathtub and downs his bottle. He shows his black teeth in booming guffaws as the water runs over his boots.

With his gun butt, Smokotin knocks off the faucets and puts them in his pocket. Pavel returns to stare at the light. The heat of the bulb on his hand brings a grin. He goes to get Konstantin to ask him to explain the light. Konstantin tells him and shows him how the light screws in and out. When he is gone Pavel with great care unscrews the bulb and puts it in his pocket, for he wants to see the light when it comes on again.

Platochuk stands in the center of the warehouse in a splendid costume with a big hat.

"It is the time of Napoleon," says Konstantin.

Nobokof grabs a costume for himself. It has a crinoline skirt and tears along the back as he puts it on. He kicks up his heels.

The men roar with laughter as each chooses a costume. Smokotin puts on a long white toga, which has a laurel wreath pinned to it. He puts the laurel wreath around his neck. Ulkyakhtakuva wears a Spanish doublet with a white ruff collar. Pavel wears a long coat of sequined mail, which has a great white cross down the front. Konstantin helps them to put on the costumes. But soon so many other soldiers are crowding in that he backs out to watch the men already parading in the street. One breaks out a concertina, and the men begin to dance.

Fires burn behind them, and to the west smoke hangs like a pall over the sprawling city that awaits them beyond. Konstantin is clapping and laughing uproariously, the only one of perhaps fifty soldiers not now wearing all or part of some colorful costume. The men are spinning and bending and leaping to the swift music.

The first shot fired pierces the heart of Konstantin. After only a flash of pain, he does not even feel the street coming to meet him.

Three other men and the concertina are shot before the company disperses and storms the building from which the firing has come.

Inside a dank room they find a boy of about fourteen, standing straight-backed before them, and a man cowering in the corner. The boy's hair falls in a long dark lock over his forehead. To the other side two women cringe. The soldiers cannot tell who has done the shooting—a search reveals no weapons. They shoot the boy and the man on the spot.

Smokotin approaches the women. One is old enough to be his mother, but has fewer wrinkles. He lifts his toga and smiles. The other, a mere girl without curve or extra flesh, screams as Pavel lifts his skirt of sequined mail and fumbles at his fly.

When they finish, Pavel cracks the older woman's skull with his rifle butt. He is still angry, for she has broken his light bulb. Last with the girl, a soldier from another unit slits her belly with his bayonet, which he has honed to a fine edge.

The men return to the street to dance. The concertina squeaks now. To enliven the dance, the men fire in the air.

Two officers come striding into them. At the end of a street a T-34 tank squats, the muzzle of its 85mm gun a black mouth over their heads. A personnel carrier and a weapons carrier move up from behind to join the tank. The men gradually stop dancing. Only their heavy breaths sound in the still air.

"What is this madness?" says the first officer.

"Clowns, dunces, fools," says the second officer.

The drunken Pavel sizes up the second officer. "The little kid is baa baa," he says.

The second officer takes a pistol from a holster and points it at Pavel's stomach. "I am Lieutenant Irena Malinovskii, First Mechanized Corps. If you wish to be dead, you will say that again. Go on, say it."

Pavel stands staring at her and says nothing.

"Men die while you play," she says. "Go forward and do your duty."

"They are without leaders," says the first officer. The fuzz on his face makes him look very young. "They have been mobilized from the farthest primitive reaches. What can you expect?"

"Beasts," she says, waving her pistol at them. "Take off those ridiculous clothes. Get up there now. I will have you shot at this very moment."

The men leave their costumes in the street and march forward sullenly.

"She-wolf," says Private Josef Sejonovitsch Smokotin.

"Bitch-dog," says Private Aleksai Andianovich Nobok-of.

"Pig," says Private Boris Platochuk.

"Goat," says Private Vasili Senovich Ulkyakhtakuva.

"Ox," says Private Boris Platochuk.

Pavel hawks up some phlegm. "Officers."

Lieutenant Malinovskii watches them turn the corner. She puts her pistol back in the holster and shakes her head at the other officer. "What is this day?" she asks. "Monday. Monday, April, I have forgotten the date. Monday. Our flag will be flying over this hole of hell by the end of the week."

"All of Berlin over there, too," says the first officer.

"Maybe," Lieutenant Malinovskii says as he strides away.

She turns once to look backward at the costumes of Caesar's legions, King Arthur's knights, Bismarck's army, the hordes of Attila the Hun and Genghis Khan, evzones of Greece, lying in the street like bits of torn flags. Her back to the tank, she spits.

A GRAND VALENTINE

A storm whips up high seas along the northwest coast, and it takes us three days to get from Portland to the Strait of Juan de Fuca between the States and Canada. A Navy destroyer can make the distance in less than a day, an automobile between breakfast and lunch, an airplane between juice and coffee. But the SS *Edmund O. Valentine* is a beat-up old Liberty ship, and with no cargo aboard she's nothing more than a big empty bucket bouncing on the troughs of waves. Between the times we spend cussing her for going backward instead of forward, we worry if she'll start coming apart. She doesn't.

As soon as we enter the Strait, the water turns silvery smooth. Gulls soar free and easy wheeling, and clouds hang white and puffy. We take an easy swing to port and head up between green islands into Haro Strait. Beyond lies the Georgia Strait and Vancouver, British Columbia, where we're scheduled to take on a load of UNRRA grain for Trieste. As we finish our first square meal since Portland, we're in a cheerful mood because we know the worst part of the trip is over right at the beginning.

A small pilot boat draws a long pencil arc toward us. The 2nd orders engines to slow and stop to await the pilot coming aboard. The 2nd isn't supposed to be on the bridge, but the captain hasn't made it out of his cabin. During the time we were in dry dock in Portland, he'd gone on a glorious toot to celebrate a divorce begun at the end of the war, and he's not finished yet. We figured him for a pretty good skipper coming up from San Francisco to Portland, but this reclusive binge has brought some changing of minds. Scuttlebutt has it he's got a woman stowed away in his cabin, but we have no proof—nobody's seen her. All we know from the steward is that the food left in front of his door keeps disappearing, and is replaced by empties from his private stock of booze.

As far as the deck crew's concerned, the 2nd, a Kings Pointer named Warden, is the only mate aboard worth his salt. Except for a few catnaps now and then, he'd stayed awake during the entire storm to keep us afloat and headed in the right direction. Now he's out on his feet, leaning over the bridge, his eyes like dabs of red lead primer.

We drop a pilot's ladder over the side as the pilot boat eases in under us. The 2nd's smile of relief relaxes us even more. We're now not only in good hands—we're in superior hands. From these little boats all over the world come stately, venerated men, master mariners wise in the ways of life and the sea, experienced in every intricacy of handling a ship in a certain waterway.

Two pilots come out of the pilot house, one short and heavy, the other tall and skinny. They're yelling at each other, chin to chin, one up, one down. Neither of them is a Billy Conn by any means, but they sure look ready to go at it.

"She's no good for you," the fat one says. "She's just stringing you along for laughs."

"What do you know, you stinking tub of lard," the skinny one says.

"I know who she's waiting for, and it isn't you, you bag of fossil bones."

We've thrown down a line for the pilot's bag, but no one pays any attention to it.

"We'll see about that," the tall one shouts and brakes against his boat rail like a huron coming in for a landing. He starts to claw his way up our ladder.

"You're too old, you're all dried up," the fat pilot shouts up. "She doesn't want no dried-up old balls."

Our pilot turns and kicks out his foot. He almost falls off the ladder. If the boat hadn't already slipped away from our side, he'd probably have gone back down the ladder and taken on the other pilot. He scrambles up and vaults from the gunwale to the deck over hands trying to help him.

"This ain't some slow old croaker, you know." He has a handsome set of teeth, but yellowed as old piano keys. He whips out a big bandanna, takes off his cap, and wipes his face. He's around sixty, flappy of movement, with a beaked nose and a bald corrugated beanie of a skull atop a white wreath of hair. The skin of his face and neck have begun to soften, but the effects of wind and sun over a span of years at sea are as ineradicable as the crackings of dried leather.

"Your bag, sir," the 3rd says, for the third time.

The old pilot whirls and waves a fist like a tomahawk. Two bright cherry spots stand out on his cheeks. The pilot boat is already beginning to make way toward a C-2 astern of us. The pilot screeches for his bag, and the boat circles back. He leans over the rail, hands cupped to his mouth. "Give me my bag, you greasy baboon."

The other pilot stands with his arms folded as the line drops over again. "Come down and get it yourself."

"I'll report you, you ape." He points to the helmsman who has come out of the pilot house. "You want to lose your . . . that's better."

The helmsman puts the bag down again, looks up, then at the fat pilot. The two pilots yell at him. The helmsman finally ties the rope to the bag and we haul it up, a shiny new cowhide Gladstone, and heavy.

"Stand off or I'll run you down," the old pilot yells. He turns to see that his bag is safe. "Can't forget my fancy duds, now can I?" He glances at a flat gold watch. "Horn knockers, lost three minutes already." The lid snaps shut with a silent tick, and he slides the watch back into his vest pocket. "Come on, laddy bucks, let's get a move on." He twists his head up in the direction of the perplexed 2nd on the bridge and shrieks, "Howdy, Cap'n. Full ahead, no time to lose." He tears up the boat deck ladder two steps at a time.

Those of us in the fo'c's'le head crew go ahead with the chief mate, while the rest follow the 3rd astern. In minutes the old tub is shearing the water like a destroyer.

The 1st scratches his head. "Must be doing twelve-fourteen knots. I didn't know she had it in her."

"We're gonna bust in half," says Ajax, an AB who kept an ear on her shuddering all during the coast trip.

One of the oilers comes topside and wanders up to the bow in search of a tool. "Them pistons is going so fast they gonna fly off and bust big holes right in our belly."

"Get back down in the hole," the 1st says. "You got no business up here."

"I can't swim," says the oiler and wanders back midships.

"The skipper ought to do something," Ajax says. "I mean it's his ship, not no John Cobb."

The 1st scratches his belly. "Hell, the Old Man don't know if we left Portland yet." He glances up at the bridge. "Well, what do you know."

The captain's standing out on the wing with the pilot. We watch him. Not standing—*leaning*. He's holding a coffee cup, and has a pleasant smile pasted on his face. Too pleasant. The 2nd is nowhere in sight.

"Give the bridge a ring and find out what lines that old coot wants out. While you're at it, try to find out what he's so all fired in a hurry about." All this comes from a bitt where the 1st sits. The less moving he has to do, the better.

Toby's manning the phone in the wheelhouse and spreads the word whenever the Old Man and the pilot stay out on the wing.

"He's got a woman waiting for him in Vancouver," Toby says.

"What the hell, that don't mean nothing," the 1st says when he hears this.

"Does to him," Toby says. "Even shows me and Klotz her picture. Got one in his wallet, and another in his suitcase. He's got it between his clothes and a slug of vitamin bottles and colognes. Looks like a drug store in there. Dame about 45 trying to look 25. Showing off her new— what do you call them things?—a strapless bra, yeah, posing in one of them, and this new dumb-looking long skirt. Not bad looking for a skinny old dame. Tells him her girlfriend took the pictures, ha. Hold it."

"Strapless bra?" Ajax says. "How can they stay up?"

The 1st scratches his ear at the news. "If that don't beat all. A strapless bra. I don't get it—ain't he ever had a woman?"

"Okay, coast is clear," Toby says. "Sure, married for thirty years, he says, most of the time at sea. His wife hangs around waiting for him to come home and settle down. So he did, starts to piloting, and right away the war busts out, so he goes back to sea. After the war he comes back to take up piloting again, and his wife ups and dies.

About as lonely, as miserable as can be, he meets up with this widow lady. Pounds his chest, says he feels younger'n anybody else aboard this ship. She's waiting for him, and nobody else, he says, nosireebob. Oops, here he comes."

The 1st scratches his belly. "If that don't beat all." He shifts his seat to the hatch to get out of the way of our work. "Yeah, better get them lines ready. We'll be easing into the dock in no time, less'n he expects us to take off and land at the airport." He scratches his jaw. "Any old salt gets himself hooked that bad is a drownded man. Best way to get along with women is to have a passel of 'em, port to port, and treat 'em all the same: mean. Then they 'preciate you."

Thornson, the carpenter, lends a hand with a hawser. "Prob'ly a slut after his nest egg. Play the poor ole sucker for all he's worth, then dump him." A speech of this length from the carpenter is unusual. He hasn't said as much in any one time since his couple of grunts in the mess the morning we signed on in San Francisco. The bosun, an old shipmate of his, says that when Thornson got back home in Oakland after his last trip he discovered that his wife's run off with a taxi driver.

"Maybe, maybe not," says Jim Stead, an OS who's got a wife and two kids down in Long Beach. "Sometimes you see a young broad hanging on some old bird's arm like it was her favorite drumstick."

Thornson hawks in disgust and leaves off to stand by at the windlass. His job at docking is to let go the anchor in case it's needed.

The pilot is skittling back and forth across the bridge as we buzz through the channel. He keeps leaning over the wing to look back at the C-2 which has drawn closer astern.

"Still talking a blue streak," Toby says between one of the flights. "Friendly old bird—not like most pilots. Tells me he grew up around here, sailed these waters as a boy before he went to sea. He's been telling the Old Man about the Murmansk run, how he lost two Libertys, both torpedoed. Gabs at the Old Man a mile a minute."

"How is the Old Man?" somebody wants to know.

"Green," Toby says.

We tear into the channel. We slow only long enough to pick up two tugs; then they have trouble keeping up with us in what little distance there is left to the piers that jut off the downtown area. His arms waving like semaphore flags, the pilot urges the tugs on. As we approach our slip, he orders a hard right rudder, and we start to nose in at good speed. We can hear all the way to the bow every command for the helmsman and the engine room. The 2nd is probably back in the wheelhouse by now to handle the telegraph.

A Liberty may be an old tub, yet she's more than a city block long. She's no motorboat to maneuver, especially when she's riding empty in a fast current and trying to dock in a four-ship slip already occupied by three others: on our starboard, a Dutch freighter, low in the water and carrying a deck load of lumber; ahead of her a Navy cargo ship; and on our port, a Victory, being loaded. It's going to be a tight squeeze, and the tugs don't have much room to operate in.

With our stem into the slip, the pilot orders engines stopped. He must have finally realized that we're going too fast. Shuddering, the ship slows, slows too quickly. The current catches us and sends our stern drifting against the Dutch freighter. We carom hard off her port side. There's a long scrunch of metal screaming against metal. From out on the wing, head twirling about like a wind-up duck, the pilot screams Slow Ahead, then countermands the order, but it's garbled because the Old Man has come to life, and he's screaming orders, too. They're both waving their arms now, and no one can tell what either one's saying. Our bow has already started to swing toward the Victory on our port. In the curve of the prow we can't see back to the stern, but we can tell that in coming away from the Dutch freighter, the *Valentine* has somehow caught part of her deck load. His back to us, the pilot is craning his head upward. Flying objects are visible against the sky, and we can hear screeches from the 3rd on the phone at the stern. "Look out, there's another one, 2x4, look out, 4x8, loo-o-o-k out, holy mackerel, must have been a 2x12."

We brace ourselves in the bow. Nothing is going to stop us from ramming the Victory. We plow into her starboard bow with a long grinding scrunch and bounce off her.

In the lull that follows, and it's only an instant, we can hear Toby's voice over the phone. "Hey, we oughta charge admission."

Easy to see what he's talking about because we're attracting rows of onlookers from the other ships. But there's only a second for us to take in the audience, and the skipper, who appears to have been struck dumb, and the old pilot, flapping his arms in a mad flight from one wing to the other. He lets go with another shriek, this one loud and clear: "Let go the starboard anchor." The carpenter, who has abandoned his post at the windlass to have a look at the point of collision against the Victory, makes a dive and lets go the brake. By then, it's too late to heed the bursting chorus of *NO*'s from the Navy ship and what sounds like *NAYN*, again and again, from the Dutch freighter, too late, because the chain is already rumbling as it pays out the plunging anchor.

For it's then the pilot hears, with us, at the same time as the anchor rumbling, a squawk of the highest intensity yet. It comes from below and he sees with us the lead tug, to that moment forgotten, butting with the persistence of a billy goat alongside our starboard bow under the anchor. She's an ancient little tug with a three-man crew. The two deck hands look up, eyes like pistol bull's-eyes, mouths open red as watermelon slices. The cries still in their throats, they leap off opposite sides of the tug and hit the water at the same instant that the flukes tear into the tug's forward deck. The helmsman, avoiding the fate accorded the last man on a vessel in distress but a bit slower getting away from the cabin, is just taking his last step when the anchor hits. Aided by its impact the way vaudeville acrobats soar off the ends of see-saw boards, he flies up over the water right in front of us. The expression on his face says to us: This can't be happening to me. Unfortunately there are no friendly shoulders to land on at the zenith of his flight, and he has nowhere else to go but back down. The anchor meanwhile rips through the deck with the ease of an axe into balsa wood—a good anchor weighing close to two tons—and takes her right down with it. Our line down to the tug jumps off her bitt. The tug sinks, glug, just like that. All that's left are the sounds of hissing as the hot stack gurgles under, and the three tug men spitting out pier water.

So fascinating is the spectacle of the disappearing tug, so colorful the oaths of the three bobbing corks, making their way to the raw planks of lumber floating around them, that nobody realizes the anchor chain is still paying out, not even Chips, who has again abandoned his post at the windlass to see what's going on. That's when the next shriek comes, this one from the 1st: "Gaw-wd. Stop anchor! We're gonna ram the dock." He makes a lunge for the windlass at the same time as the pilot's cry to back engines. But all too late. The *Valentine* keeps moving forward. Implacably. Somebody grabs the fog horn, probably Toby would do a fool thing like that, and starts blasting away. To the tune of the fog horn and splintered pilings and ripping metal, we slice our way into the head of the dock. The collision is but an anticlimax, and the 1st, who winds up on the seat of his pants in a scupper, slowly passes a hairy hand over his face.

A pall of silence descends over the pier as the fog horn lets up. The pilot, holding the sides of his head at the hair, is just coming to a stop from his latest flight. The skipper still looks frozen solid. Back along the way, the three tug men, hugging planks, are reaching for lines with all the eagerness of hungry trout.

Then jeers start from the Navy ship, like "Wanna try for a downtown parking lot?" and "Got any more of that kickapoo juice you guys been guzzling?" When Thornson yells that he's going to come over and haul their ashes if they don't lay off, one swabby yells back, "Think your seeing-eye dog can make it?"

Toby's voice comes over the phone. "Looks like Don Juan's going to be a little late for his date."

Thornson harrumphs.

"Purty good day's work, I'd say," Toby adds.

"Least we didn't kill nobody," Ajax says.

It takes us a while to back out of the slot we've made in the dock. In the silence that falls as we wait to see what might happen in this manuever, we can hear commands from a ship being nudged carefully into place a pier away. The voice is a familiar one: loud, but now cold, mechanical, precise.

As for the *Valentine*, we make it into position and tie up. Then we start to lower the gangplank. Through a crowd of office girls and dock workers who have gathered out on the dock to stare at us, comes the other pilot. He surveys the damage and shakes his head, scanning the bridge for the old pilot.

"Satisfied now?" he yells up.

The voice from above is not the old pilot's; rather, it's Toby's: "Aww, go soak your fat gut."

The fat pilot's mouth stays open, then, jaw reddening, clamps shut. He scans the bridge in search of his newest enemy. Not finding either, he stomps away, and we hear chortling from up on the bridge.

While we're getting the gangplank down, there's a jostling along the passageway, followed by the high-pitched voice of the pilot: "Gangway. All right, laddy bucks, let's hop to, hop to." Behind him comes Toby, then Klotz, the helmsman.

The old pilot's eyes gleam wide and bright, as shiny as pearls, the skin fever-cherried along the cheeks. Wisps of hair hang over his ears. Nobody has his bag. Drumming his bony fingers on the rail, with a look in his face of something rich and strange, he mutters, "No difference, makes no difference at all, nosireebob."

He jumps before the gangplank has touched all the way down and, pushing his way through the crowd, makes his way to a phone booth at the head of the dock. He's taking steps like a sandhill crane getting ready to take off. His erect shoulders start to slump a bit as he nears the phone booth. It has been knocked askew and is at the point of falling on its back, doors up. He pushes it upright but still it leans on its side. He steps inside anyway, and the door unhinges and closes with the loud *skrung-THUNK* of a cage banging shut.

We gather by the rail forward of midships and look at the crowd starting to drift away. A few of the office girls linger. Ajax is winking. The bosun has a habit when he's idle of twirling the hair between his collarbones with his thumb and index finger, and he's busy twirling now. Toby's smiling at them. The girls look back over their shoulders as they walk away.

"Ooooo-eee, we're gonna get to know Vancouver like we knew Portland," Ajax says with a grin, waving a limp hand in front of himself.

"You said it," Toby agrees. "We'll be here a month of Sundays getting this mess straightened out."

"What's going to happen to the old guy?" Jim Stead asks.

Thornson draws his index finger across the underside of his chin.

"Yeah, his ass is in a sling all right," Toby says. "Wish it was the Old Man instead of him—maybe it will be. Who's going to be able to figure out who's to blame and who ordered what?"

"Where *is* the Old Man?" Jim Stead asks.

"Where do you think?" Klotz says, tippling his thumb.

We look up. Only the 2nd is on the bridge, leaning over, pinching his eyes and the bridge of his nose, a bewildered sad smile on his face.

"Yeah, count on being here a spell," Toby says, "what with the inspectors and claims adjusters and lawyers and shipping line execs and the port authorities and the Navy brass and the Dutchies and the whozits all over the place, with their clipboards and their cameras and their tape measures."

The phone booth door creaks. The old pilot is still inside, back turned, shoulders slumped. A cover of shadow spreads over the phone booth.

"The whole kaboodle right on top of his head," Ajax says.

"Love's a funny thing," Toby says.

"What makes you say that?" Jim Stead asks.

"Can't you see—it just busted his ass," Toby says.

But it doesn't. Early that evening the widow lady comes down to the dock. We like her. She's no Queen of the May, by a long shot, scrawny and bidding hello to 50, but she's a nice lady, grave and steady looking, yet with a winkle at the eye that says, well, what the hell. As he sees her, cobwebs leave the old pilot's eyes, and he suddenly grows taller by five full inches. When she takes his hand, we can see it fits just right. It's plain she has a lot of love stored up in her, maybe enough to get him through this mess, which she dismisses with one utterance, "What a grand Valentine you brought." We look in on them now and then through portholes of the mess, not so much to spy on them as maybe to protect them or to admire them. They sit there holding hands, knobby knees stuck together under the table, while the inspectors and the appraisers and the whozits crawl over the ships and the dock like rats.

THE SACRIFICE

"They are not satisfied," says the old-young matador, testing the sword blade against the barrera and squinting up into the crowd. He is not old in years, only thirty, but he has been in the ring half his life.

"The vultures," mutters Julio Guarda, his manager. He spits and with his foot smoothes over a little mound of dirt against the fence. Spitting gives him pleasure but he's very clean about it. He wipes his fleshy face with a soggy handkerchief and, shifting the stump of his cigar to the other side of his mouth, he adds: "They are never satisfied."

There is never an empty seat in the plaza when the name **PRINCIPE** stands in fresh shadows at the head of the posters all over town. The crowd waits for the matador to make his final appearance of the afternoon. On the sunny side of the arena, the last bull also waits, waits to be killed, or to kill. Earlier the crowd leaped up in a body when Calixto, the young Andalusian, was cartwheeled high in the air while executing a molinete with the second bull. But word has come from the infirmary that he was not badly hurt. Now he's being patched up to fight another day.

"Something is going to happen to me out there today," says the matador. His voice is quiet, tired. He takes a drink of water handed to him by the manager and turns to rinse his mouth.

"Nonsense, Principe," says the manager, raising his arm to clap him on the back, but not touching him. "You will make a perfect kill."

"He is made for you," says the matador's swordhandler, a seam-faced, stringy little man, who stands on his other side. His name is Francisco but he is called Mono. He shifts his weight from his withered right leg, the result of a cornada that ended his career as a novice, and looks across the ring at the bull which stands pawing the sand and shaking the cluster of banderillas lodged in its back. "He is made for you," he repeats, "a mountain—a magnificent animal."

"I will kill him," says the matador. "It is not that I feel."

The manager and the swordhandler frown.

The matador continues, with the trace of a smile on his sad, thin-lipped mouth: "No, there is no fear this time. But we see if today I am to die, too." He takes his hat and the muleta and turns to face the ring. Then, looking over his shoulder with the same slight smile, he adds: "You are like the pallbearers, you two. You must learn to smile."

The matador steps out of the shelter and looks up at the judge who nods his permission for the kill. A stillness settles over the plaza, though more slowly on the sunny side where bets are still being passed along with wine jugs. Pulls on the squishy, small-necked jugs are longer than usual when Principe appears in the plaza, and when his bull is good and the capework finishes, the pulls become even longer. Bets are largely statistical. How many linked pases naturales will the torero make? How long before he will drop to his knees? From there, how many farol passes? After a while, all count is lost anyway and no one ever bothers to collect anything.

Principe walks along the fence. His pale blue and gold suit turns bright when he steps out of the shadow into the splash of light. He raises his montera high and, slowly turning right and left, salutes the plaza. Then he tosses the hat over his shoulder up into the crowd. The muleta draped over the sword, he strides toward the center of the ring, calling softly but clearly to the bull. The cape hangs limp to the ground. His lips hardly part as he mutters: good, still no wind.

Immense, powerful, still brave, Locomotora, number 38 from the feared Azorín stock, raises its yellowish white horns. Then, like an explosion of blackness rocketing toward a target, the bull charges. Principe does not move as the bull hurtles past, the horns passing inches away from him. The muleta ripples up and flutters down. The bull wheels and charges again. Principe executes a series of standing passes, each more intricate and daring than the last, all of them, including two of his own invention, deceptively casual while he continues to control the animal. And yet each time the horns graze his body.

This calm in the Pass of Death distinguishes Principe: always inviting tragedy but somehow, save for the four times in his career when he has been gored, escaping it. He does not work in the neo-classic manner—he *is* the neo-classic manner: all severity and starkness. He was born there, an American correspondent once wrote of him, born there in front of a bull, and in another passage the same admirer remarked: "I think he learned his trade with a diaper and a safety pin." But where Principe came from they never heard of diapers.

The shape of the bullring being what it is, the plaza now funnels itself into the bullfighter below, as into the aperture of a bottomless hourglass. When the Olés become a chant, he draws them further; when they become a onethroated roar, he draws them further yet. When the Olés become a plea, an exhortation to stop, for the love of God and Heaven and the Merciful Mother, he sucks them ever downward. Then he drops to his knees to drain them more, to make them forget to wave their handkerchiefs, to make the musicians forget to play their Dianas. The co-owners of the ring, who are brothers, stop dwelling on the corrida's receipts. Even the president in his box, notorious for his impassiveness in the face of the worst event, sits with his mouth flopped open like a guppy's.

This is the genuflection of man to beast, afarolado de rodillas; what in the plaza they have come to see and not to see. It has been said that the pass on the knees is not a true maneuver, only a frill. Principe has made it an artistic part of his repertoire by reducing it to its essence. It has become a maneuver to be watched only by a hardy people, for over the years it has burst the hearts and numbed the brains of a score of spectators. No one has ever asked him how many times he has died down there in the sand in the late afternoon executing it.

Again the animal slams past Principe, kneeling with the piece of cloth, hardly larger than a handkerchief, held out and up limply from his side. The matador feels the horn graze his head as the cape swirls and leaps but he knees around to take another charge. The bull twists and thunders by once more.

Principe whispers across the sand. "You, my lovely big train, bring me the package again."

More slowly, from less distance, the animal charges, winded and weak by now from the rent of the lance in the withers and the sting of the banderillas in the back. In and away, the ebb and flow of the package. And then again, still more slowly, in and away, and around, like a great ebony top whirling about an axis of gold. Each time the bull leaves a memento of itself, a swipe of spittle, a swatch of blood, a tuft of hair, but takes nothing for itself from the tormenter, for it has not yet learned the cloth is not the true enemy, not yet.

After the twelfth, perhaps the twentieth, or it might have been the hundredth pass, for all the plaza knows in the dizziness of its fascination and excitement, the bull stands directly in front of the matador. The eyes of the man and of the animal fasten upon one another, bodies transfixed, as if turned to stone.

"I am there in your eyes, Toro," the matador whispers, feeling for this bull the braveness and frustration of the thousand bulls he has killed, himself transported to an ecstasy of his own mastery over primeval force. "It is the reflection of us all," Principe whispers again. But he is tired, and one cannot be tired and fight bulls.

From behind the shelter the manager murmurs, "No, Principe. Amigo verdadero. Vaquero. You fight too close." He works his mouth but cannot spit. He wrings his sweaty hands and says at the swordhandler but not to him, "Madre mía, why does he always fight too close and too long? Does he expect to hypnotize that cathedral?"

"It is what they want of him," replies the swordhandler, sucking in his breath and holding it, without removing his eyes from the spectacle before him.

Alongside the matador, the bull remains dead-still, the massive head downward, the right horn a shadow away from coppery flesh. Beneath the cape the man and the animal are as occult as two lovers, hidden.

The bull shudders. By design or chance, the horn moves in and up and out, deftly, almost delicately. The tip of the horn enters the eye socket of the matador, clean and sharp, like an ice pick. Then a twist, and the eye of the matador, the left eye, is plucked out and falls on the sand.

An explosive agony shoots through the matador, as though his head and body are eviscerated with one slash of a straight-edge razor. But when that searing black moment is gone, he feels little pain. The rivulet down his cheek might be blood or sweat, the matador doesn't know and it doesn't matter. What matters is finishing his bull.

Up in the plaza, they are not aware. Behind the barrera, they know. Julio Guarda lets out a squeal and starts into the ring, followed by the swordhandler and others of the cuadrilla. Stumbling to his feet, the sword blade gleaming as he whirls, Principe waves them away. His lips say if you come here I will kill you too. Frightened of him now—the swordhandler moaning from a suddenly erupted pain in his leg—the bullfighter's cuadrilla leaves him alone there, they who have seen him hurt before but never like this.

Principe readies the sword, and sighting the bull through a drifting fog of vision, he says for the bull and not for himself, "Brujo, the pity is that you do not know more about the eye and the tooth. Love and pain is like this, Brujo. Now, come to me, Torazo, come to me, it is the end."

The bull can hook and finish its tormenter because now it knows the way but it comes straight as an express train down a grade. The lowered right horn skimming by him as he lunges, Principe buries the sword to the hilt at the precise spot instinctively aimed for in the bull's humped shoulders. The package dies well, instantly, off the ground, falling on its back with its hoofs straight up.

In that instant, Principe comes back to the sand from wherever he has been, from whatever has made him kill the bull. With a sob and a fumbling lunge, he picks up the eye and holds it in his palm. It lies there, light, whole, ugly. His empty hand covers his mutilated socket and from his lips comes a cry like a lost child's from across a lake at night. His face twisted in horror, he takes in with one rotation of his head the plaza, struck to dumb silence by his action, and the rim of the blue sky beyond. Then he throws the eye high into the plaza.

Its landing is like that of a stone tossed by the same child into the water that same afternoon. Up there, a scramble follows for this object, unknown but priceless. A shriek heralds its discovery. Sounds move out and away, widening like ripples, the shriek to a scream to cries to gasps. And gasps become the tormented throat of the plaza.

Below, men gorge into the ring from behind the barrier, the manager and the swordhandler sobbing prayers on the run, while the figure of gold and pale blue and streaks of red walks a broken path into the shadow, with nothing more to give for this time.

LOCKE-HAVEN AT LARGE

Me and Jamie just come down from the overpass on the way to Blissvale, this neighboring burg where he lives, when the marshal got shot. Dead. I seen it all. I was riding on the handlebars and had me a front row seat.

First I see this little yellow house on the corner where a guy is on the front porch beating on the door with his fist. He's yelling, I waited long enough, and he's raising his foot to bust down the door. I get me just a glimpse of two people hightailing it out the back. They're going past the garbage cans, a guy wearing a T shirt and levis slung so low they like to fall off, and a woman trailing long pink veils so's you can see the crack of her can, and they're gone.

Meantime me and Jamie come closer and I see this black car pull up on the opposite side of the street where there's a vacant lot, and two men get out. I know who they are because Jamie showed them to me one time when we were going over to his house to have a war. They were sitting out in front of the Blissvale jail, which is nothing but a big square box with a few bars on a window and a leanto office alongside of it that says Marshal.

So here he comes, walking tall across the street, with his thumbs hooked in his belt. His deputy next to him is starting to take his gun out of his holster. The guy on the porch is just splintering the door.

The marshal calls out, Harvey, Harvey, what's all this here fuss?

The guy on the porch turns, his hands down at his sides, and steps over to the edge and up comes this big pistol straight out and he fires twice. The marshal goes down like a plank falling straight backward and bounces and sends up some dust in the middle of the street and lays there stiff, except for his boot that jumps a couple of times and then stops. The second shot hits the deputy in the arm, and I see his pistol go flying through the air and he falls to his knees.

The guy with the gun steps off the porch onto a yellow patch of grass and looks over at the marshal. I see now he's a pale, sandy haired guy wearing a washed out khaki shirt and pants, and his eyes are kind of vacant and strange. Except for those eyes, he's just a plain ordinary looking guy. You wouldn't take him to be nobody that just killed somebody, and maybe more next. Me and Jamie are by now stopped right in front of him alongside the marshal and we hear the deputy groaning. The guy starts to raise his gun again, but it don't come up very high, so to tell the truth I'm not sure whether he's going to shoot me and Jamie or not. It all happened so fast, less than a minute, so we didn't have much time to get scared. He squints at me and his mouth twitches, but he don't say anything. He just turns and walks up the porch and on in the house through the splintered door.

I'm off the handlebars and Jamie drops his bike right there in the street and we bend over the marshal. There's a hole in his shirt pocket, a pink circle around it about the size of a silver dollar. He hasn't bled hardly at all, except what is underneath his back, staring straight up at us, and his mouth fixed just like he's still saying the last word he ever was to say, and that was fuss. The handcuffs at his side are flashing in the sun, and his gun is still strapped peaceable like in its holster.

The deputy is still on his knees, groaning, my God, my God, my arm, and trying to hold the elbow with his good hand. His arm is a mess and bleeding bad. He's got his teeth together and the sweat's running off his face. He says, Your shirt, boy, your shirt. I'm shaking some but I get my shirt off quick. I twirl it around like a snake and I wrap it around his arm above the elbow and I squeeze and he's grunting, That's it, that's it.

People are starting to come out from their houses, and two cars going by the T intersection slow down and stop. Somebody says he tried to call the marshal but couldn't raise him, and Jamie says, That's him there. Another man says he called the Marchildon police and they'll be along any minute. A woman says, Where's he gone? and Jamie says, In the house, and the folks get jittery like they're going to get shot up but it appears to me he's already lit out.

We hear the sirens wailing, and then the police are swarming all around. They're from the county sheriff's and the Marchildon police department. Two ambulances screech up on the Marchildon side where the street's paved. The police are jawing at each other, paying no attention to me and Jamie who were maybe the only ones to see the shooting. A crowd is closed in around the marshal. Then the ambulance drivers start to jawing too when somebody asks them why they don't help the deputy.

My contract says the city limits of Marchildon, mister. So's his. The Blissvale Board don't like nobody poking in their business.

Where's Bowen?

Out on call, I expect.

So you mean you ain't going to take Stats here. Hellfire, he's bleeding all over the place.

I told you, we can't touch him but halfway this side of the street.

The deputy is muttering cuss words not fit for the ladies to hear.

One of the ambulance drivers bends down talking to the deputy, elbowing me aside and waving everybody away so's the deputy can get up and walk over to the middle of the street, which he does, kind of staggering. He gets in the ambulance, and off they go. I'm not worried about my shirt, except what my ma will say when I tell her I haven't got it anymore.

The sheriff himself has pulled up, and him and two policemen get to arguing over who's in charge. The other police start to asking questions about who did the shooting and where the shots come from.

A gray haired guy wearing an apron says, Harvey Locke-Haven shot him. He spells out the name good on account of he runs Pop's Grocery Store around the corner that gives credit. He says, His house is right there, the Mrs. house. Don't worry, he ain't there no more. I seen him going past my place, toting his gun too, like he don't care who sees it.

Anybody in the house?

Not no more. He come to kill Virgie, I reckon. She took off.

While the police and the sheriff are getting a description of him, I try to say something a couple of times but nobody pays any attention to me. Jamie neither. Pretty soon the police tell everybody to go on home.

Aren't you going to pick up the marshal? I pipes up.

You mind your mouth, boy, says a policeman, the one that's holding the deputy's gun.

He's got more sense than you, a woman says.

We can't touch him, ma'am. We ain't allowed to.

Well I never.

We called your mayor. He's coming and settle it.

Well, Mrs. Preece's not going to take to his being left there in the dirt.

Two little ones, no more than babies, another woman says.

You boys get, another policeman says. His fingers are pinching my arm. Your pa ought to take a strap to you, poking around dead bodies.

But, mister.

Let's go, Jamie, I says.

I don't feel much like going to his house anymore. Besides I got to get the blood off me. So I tells Jamie I'll see him later and head on home. At the top of the overpass I stop and catch my breath. I wonder if those two people are still running, like I was. I look back over where Blissvale is and bet myself they're long gone out of that rinky burg. I don't see anybody running in Marchildon, far as I can see past the railroad yards over trees and roofs. There's lots of places to run, though, clean up to the foothills. I can see the college up on the bench to one side. Slopes on the other side are mostly bare, except for some new houses and a big ugly water tank that looks like a toadstool. Farther down I can see the top of the VA hospital where my ma works. Maybe Locke-Haven is already hiding out or maybe he's strolling along somewheres downtown easy as you please. I get to wondering what he's thinking after going and killing the marshal who knew him because he called him by his name, Harvey, Harvey, what's all this here fuss?

I run a block and walk a block all the rest of the way. Our Chevy's out in the front. When I left, Ma was canning peaches, so I guess she's still at it. Nitwit's helping her.

I don't know how Ma's going to take to the news because shooting and stuff like that drive her batty. She don't allow me to have any play guns, let alone a real one. She don't even want me to go to movies where there's any shooting. War pictures she hates most of all. I see them anyways, I just don't tell her. She feels the way she does on account of my dad and her dad. We're jinxed is the reason. They were both killed being in wars. Me and Otto figure there's no stopping the way she feels, so we just let her go ahead and be crazy about this one thing.

The smell from the kitchen spreads clear up front to the porch. Pots and kettles are bubbling and snorting, and steam is rolling around like smoke. Ma started out super efficient, but looks to me like things got out of control. There's shiny peaches stacked up in bowls, and peels and pits slopping over newspapers, and mason jars and lids and red rings and pans and funnels and strainers and big spoons and junk like that scattered all over the counters and the sink and even on top of the fridge, and sugar spilling out of a sack, and lugs tossed around by the door where I'm standing. Leave it to Nitwit and she'll turn any place into a disaster area in no time.

Where's your shirt? Ma says, just glancing at me. She's got sweat on her forehead, which is very rare for her.

I lost it, I says.

Lost it?

Lucky for me she's got her hands too full to raise the roof. I says to her, On account of the man that got shot.

Give Nora that potholder there, Ma says.

I play me a tune with a kitchen knife on the mason jars that were turned upside down on towels all around my end of the counter. I start to tell them again about the marshal, but Nitwit sticks her big nose in.

Watch what you're doing, she says. You want to give us botchism.

What? I says.

Botchism—it's a disease that creeps into the bottles from creeps like you.

Nora, my mother says.

Well, I don't want his dirty filthy little hands all over what's going into my mouth, Nitwit says.

Which is big enough to hold a piano, I says. While she's thinking of something to say back, I tell Ma I remember reading about this botchism. There was this whole family sitting around eating one day from a jar just like this, and they were all croaked, stone dead. At the funeral parlor they had to bust open their jaws to get out the spoons. I get me another knife, the flat chrome kind that bounces good on a pot, and I plays me some more beat working over to the canisters, a regular Gene Krupa.

Chip, please, Ma says.

You should have seen that pistol, I says. Kapoom, kapoom.

Take that lid off, Nora, Ma says, and then she says to me, Why don't you go out and play some more?

Oh Mama, how could you have had him? Nitwit says, her upper lip curled up so's she looks like a wart hog.

Not me, you, I says.

You ought to be in the zoo, she says.

Children, please, Ma says. She reaches over for my drumsticks and says, You want to put me in the asylum?

I was about to say sis there was the one that belonged in the booby hatch, it was right at the tip of my tongue, then I remember the time Ma hit me. We were having a big fight and I yelled at her she belonged in the booby hatch with the other loonies she was taking care of and, whap, she gave it to me right across the face. It didn't hurt me none, except to sting a little, but it hurt her something terrible because she started to bawl. She told me she was sorry she smacked me but she didn't want me to talk about the soldiers that way. She was working in the Psycho ward at the time.

I says, I been trying to tell you for a half hour. Don't you want to hear about the marshal getting killed? I seen it with my own eyes.

Saw, Nitwit says.

Aw, go suck your tit, I says.

Truman Mackie, Ma yells.

I did, I seen him shot right through the heart, I says.

My sister gives me this look like I'm an insect and she's the DDT. So I plays my ace in the hole.

How'd you like to bet $2.45? I says.

I go to my room and get my jar off my bookcase and come back and kick a lug out of the way and I dump my money upside down on the floor and I says, Well, come on, big mouth, put your money where your big fat mouth is.

I didn't play my cards right. Too eager. I could see right away ole sis was going to chicken out.

Ma looks at me for the first time, I mean really looks at me, and that's when I guess she sees the blood which is mostly smeared around my side. She puts down the pot she's holding and turns off the stove.

She takes me in the bathroom and flips down the lid of the can. Sis follows like a big dumb sheepdog. Ma's on her knees washing me off and I'm on the throne, for once getting the kind of attention I deserve. When Ma's mouth isn't hung open, she's saying, Terrible, Terrible, as I'm telling her what happened. Ole sis has got her yap closed, which is a rare event around my house. When I tell Ma about the tourniquet, she stands there holding this bloody wash rag and her eyes get all shiny and she gives me a hard squeeze and tells me she's very proud and then she apologizes for paying more mind to the peaches than to me. But when I get to talking about the guy that did the shooting, her face gets all squinched up and she says, Oh no, soon as I give his name. I ask her what's the matter, and sis says, Do you know him, Mama?

She's at the sink watching the pink come out of the rag and she says, Yes, very well. He's been a patient. The poor man. She turns and asks, Does Otto know?

I tell her I don't think so.

Go over and tell him, Chip, will you please? Ask him to come over, if he wants to, Mary, too.

How come, Ma?

Otto knows him. We were all in school together. He knew your dad, too.

So I go over to find Otto, who's our next-door neighbor. He's about the best friend I got, except for Jamie. It was him that told me exactly how my dad got killed. He didn't give me a bunch of baloney about his being a hero. They were both in the same artillery unit, which was practicing up for going to North Africa, but Otto was away that day hauling off garbage cans on a work detail. It might just as well have been my dad in the truck and Otto at the gun, but it didn't happen that way. A soldier did something stupid to a shell and it blew up. My dad and six other men got blown up, including the one that hit the shell with a wrench. One soldier, who was on the other side of the sandbags, lived to tell about it, but his hearing was bunged up for ever more.

Whenever I go to Otto's, I check first in his garage where he's got this workshop in the back. His whole house and half of ours is filled with furniture he's made. He's in there, all right, so I tell him about the marshal and the deputy and this Locke-Haven and he puts down the shelf he's fitting into a bookcase and sits down and watches me real close. I got to say this about Otto, he listens, which is very unusual because he's a teacher over in Marchildon high school. All the teachers I know do most of the talking and all you do is sit and listen.

He wipes his hands on a towel and smoothes down his hair, which is getting thin on top, and goes in to get Mary. I'm glad to hear their daughters are gone over at their grandma's. They got these two dippy girls named Iona and Olive, and they look just like they sound. They pal around with my sister, which is okay by me as long as they stay out of my hair.

We talk a lot about interesting things, like history, which is the subject he teaches. There's no man alive knows more about wars than he does. We been talking the past week about the new one that just started in Korea. I been to his school where he's showed me maps and layouts of battles in the Civil War and the Revolutionary War and the War of 1812 and the Spanish American War and the Mexican War and World War One and World War Two. I'm most interested in One and Two because they're the ones my grandad and my dad died in. Dying's another thing me and Otto talk about. I'm very interested in dying, not personally, naturally. Those are about my favorite subjects, history and dying. Otto says seems that's all there is, wars and dying in them. He says that's no way for a kid to grow up, from one war to the next. The bad part is somebody's got to do the fighting when the time comes, he says, and it's always kids. He says I'm lucky I don't have to worry about getting in this new one because I'm too young. Being born when I was, which is August 31, 1939, was why I didn't know my dad because he got killed when I was three. My sister says she remembers him, but I know she's fibbing. She was only six, and hasn't got that good of a memory.

Mary comes out, drying her hands on a dish towel, and then me and Otto wait for her to run back in and get her dumb cigarettes. They come over in the house and Ma gives them some coffee and me and sis some milk and they start to jawing about this marshal getting shot. They don't know him or the deputy, but they know a lot about this Locke-Haven. Ma drags out her old high school annual and there he is all right, looking at the birdie. He's got dimples and a big grin and wrote under his name is (Peaches and Cream). It's the same book that's got my dad. It says under his name (U.S. Senator). Ma's name was Elizabeth Huff back then, and it says under hers (Carole Lombard). Otto's is the very last picture (Salt of the Earth). Mary's picture isn't there because she's from another town, same as this Virgie they keep talking about.

Otto's curious about what happened since the shooting, so he calls up this friend he's got on the police force that tells him they haven't caught Locke-Haven, but they've blocked off the roads leading out of Marchildon-Blissvale, and they're combing the streets and searching the bus station and the train station. They picked up his wife and they're keeping her under guard. Otto smiles at what he says about her clothes. They never did find her boyfriend, and Otto says he probably ran off. She said his name was George Byron, which makes Otto smile again. Otto says he figures Harvey come to kill his wife because of this other guy. But Ma says there's other reasons. So I ask her what they are.

Ma beats around the bush telling me the war got him all mixed up and he's not always right in the head. When I ask why, Otto says, Too much combat, mean wounds, getting lost for a long time on the wrong side.

Mary blows out a big puff of smoke, hacking away, and says, Being married to Virgie was just as bad as the war. Liz, you remember how she kept calling you when he was missing, wondering why she hadn't got her money?

Ma sips her coffee and says, Uh huh.

What money? I says.

The GI insurance, Otto says.

I know about the GI insurance because that's what Ma used to buy our house.

The poor man, my mother says.

What do you keep saying that for? I says.

He didn't come back the same man, Otto says.

At least he came back, my sister says.

That's about the first smart thing I ever heard her say. Sometimes, hellfire, I actually like her. If only she wasn't such a birdbrain most of the time.

Ma tells about how he was a patient off and on at the hospital. He'd have bad spells and then he'd be all right and they'd let him go. I'm surprised at Ma because she almost never talks about the patients. Once in a great while she'll maybe say something about a vegetable with nothing but tubes stuck in him or a paraplegic and like that. One thing gets her real mad and that's when some disabled vet gets himself all spiffed up for a visit and his wife or his girlfriend don't show up. She don't like this Virgie because that's what happened to Harvey. Now I'm really surprised at Ma because she's always drumming into me and sis that if you don't have something good to say about somebody then don't say anything.

Why would he stay married to her? my sister wants to know.

He loved her, Ma says.

My sister says, Well, she didn't love him so there was no reason for her to.

The mailman brought her the reason every month, Mary says, lighting up another of her dumb cigarettes.

For a while what they talk about isn't very interesting. Then Otto brings up something that perks me up. It's about this Locke-Haven going to the college. It's not only interesting, it's sad. He had the GI Bill of Rights and even if he was not right in the head and full of shrapnel scars and pins and bolts they let him go. Otto already went to the college before the Army and then afterward he was there learning how to be a teacher. One day, Otto says, a physics teacher was demonstrating gravity and soon as these objects started to fall Harvey grabbed himself around the ears and dove under a desk. Another time a girl laughed at him and next day he come to school in his full dress uniform with all his ribbons and medals on. The worst part come about a year later when he set off a dynamite blast up in the hills back of the college. I remember people talking about it when I was a little kid, wondering if it was an atom bomb test. I sure didn't know this was the same guy. Anyways, nobody got hurt. All he did was knock out a jillion windows, but they kicked him out of the college. He went back to the hospital for a while and then when he got out he seemed all right, but they wouldn't let him back in school. He'd get on a suit and a tie and take a briefcase and go sit in the library or the student union. He would read there by the hour, Otto says. He'd say he was a graduate student, but you could tell by his grammar that he wasn't. Boy, him sitting there like that really hits me.

I look off in the direction of the college. Off to one side of Otto's chimney I can see part of this new dormitory that's being built up there.

That's prob'ly where he is, I says.

Otto comes over and looks down at me.

Oh what does he know the little—

Be still, Nora, for once, Ma says.

Right there was about my championship day, seeing the lid squashed down on her pumpkin head. She starts to sulk but nobody's paying any attention to her.

What makes you say that? Otto says.

I says, Stands to reason. Him carrying a briefcase and wanting to be at the college that bad. Well, he's running and got no place to go. That's where I'd go. Find me an empty building. It isn't any more than a mile, a mile and a half, from where he done the shooting. He could have made it easy.

Otto paces up and down and then he says to Ma, You know, the boy may be right.

He calls up his friend again at the police station and asks about seeing the chief. He hangs up and says, He's out but he'll be back in a while. Come on, Chip, you and I are going for a ride downtown, if it's okay with your mother.

She says she has to get back to her peaches before she goes to work. Mary asks if she can help. They decide they'll listen to the radio while they're working and see what it says on the news. Ma's looking so sad. When I try to cheer her up, she says she can't help it—she's feeling very bad about the marshal's family. She gives me a hug and tells me she's glad I'm safe.

I get myself a shirt on and comb my hair and me and Otto take off for the police station.

By the time the chief gets back it's already dark. Me and Otto don't mind waiting because the foyer has got interesting glass cases filled with guns and blackjacks and brass knuckles and knives. The chief takes us in his office. He looks tired and keeps rubbing his blue whiskers. I didn't see him at the shooting. Otto asks about Locke-

Haven, and the chief says they haven't seen hide nor hair of him. Otto tells him how he knew Harvey, then looking over at me he tells him what I said about the college. The chief stops rubbing his beard and says, Humm. He takes a slow spin in his chair and peeks out between his venetian blinds.

Like he's thinking out loud he mutters to himself, could be, could be, and it's a long shot, and too risky at night. He swings around and says, If he's up there, he's got the jump on us. We'd be sitting ducks with lights. I don't like the odds. He's too good a shot.

He thinks some more, swinging in his chair from side to side, then he comes around and sits on his desk, swinging his leg, and says, I'll try and find a couple men to keep an eye on the campus tonight. If Harvey's in that dorm and hasn't made a move by tomorrow, we'll search it first thing in the morning. Good thing it'll be Sunday, won't be any workmen around. Like I say, it's a long shot, but we got nothing to lose trying it.

Could I go with you, chief? Otto says.

We don't want anybody getting hurt, Mr. Zundell.

I might be able to stop somebody from getting hurt, Otto says.

The chief can't stop Otto from going along if he wants to, and tells him what time the police will be leaving in the morning.

Can I come too? I says.

The chief looks at Otto and says, I can't be responsible for a ten-'leven year old boy. His mother'd have a fit.

Otto says, He'd stay out of the way.

The chief don't like the idea, but he don't say yes and he don't say no. When we're going out, he ruffles my head and asks me if I want to be a policeman when I grow up.

I says, Not after what I seen today.

Me and Otto are glad that Ma's going to be on the night shift so's she wouldn't know I'd be gone in the morning. Otto don't like not telling her, but he comes around to a very sensible conclusion, which I figured out myself back when I was a little kid, and that is, what she don't know won't hurt her.

On account of sis is sleeping over with Olive and Iona in their back yard, Ma says it's okay if I sleep at the Zundells too. That way she wouldn't have to worry. I calls up Jamie on the sly and ask him if he wants to come in the morning, but he's going fishing with his dad. I don't sleep none too good that night. I keep thinking about this Locke-Haven hiding out in that building. Probably shaking in his boots. And then I get to thinking about him not being there. I mean, he might be in the next county by now, and I was the one swore up and down I knew where he was. I'm glad to feel Otto's hand on my shoulder waking me and the light come. He's drinking some coffee and gives me some milk and a doughnut. We tiptoe around so's not to wake up Mary.

Out on the front porch Otto flips open the Sunday paper and looks at the headlines. There in big words it says **LOCKE-HAVEN AT LARGE**, along with other headlines about the marshal killed and the deputy shot. There's pictures of all three of them, Harvey in his Army uniform. He don't look any more like the washed out looking guy I seen than he did when he was (Peaches and Cream). I glance at the rest of the page. It's got a bunch of stuff about Korea, U.S. troops starting to fight, something about Suwon and Taejon, plans for draft. Otto puts down the paper and we get in his car and take off.

I ask, How come he's got that thing between his name, Locke-Haven?

A hyphen. That's a strange story, Chip. You're going to wonder about grownups, as if you didn't already. His mother's name before she was married was Locke, his father was Haven. The mother insisted he have her name too. Well, when he was about your age his folks split up and fought over who was going to get him. His mother was going to get rid of the Haven, his dad was going to get rid of the Locke.

So who got him?

Neither one. His mother married somebody else and her new husband didn't want him, and his dad got married too, and he didn't want him either. Harvey was raised by his aunt, and kept both names.

If it'd been me I'd have changed my name to Joe Doe or something, I says.

Three patrol cars are purring in front of the station. The chief comes out and waves at Otto, and we follow them up to the college. I'm not used to getting up this early, but I like it on account of the morning is so quiet and pretty and cool. The chief picks up his two men that have been keeping watch, and then heads for the dormitory as the most likely place where Locke-Haven might be. It's a big long building, three stories, all the walls up and everything, but the roof's not finished yet and just the frames are in for the doors and windows. Up ahead there's stacks of lumber and girders and a couple big yellow machines and a pile of sand. Before we get to them, the chief pulls up in trees that are off to the side. Otto tells me to stay put where I can see, but I'm not to come any closer, and him and the police start for the building.

It don't take but a couple of minutes to find out Locke-Haven's there all right. I hear a shot. I find out later a policeman named Hackett got a finger shot off. He must have been wearing a rabbit's foot because he could have been dead. He was walking up toward the building on the back side with his gun in front of his chest and this one shot hits him in the finger and drives the gun right into his chest, which was bruised real bad, but the bullet ricocheted off.

The police start shooting and then stop on account of they don't know where Locke-Haven is inside. Soon as the shooting stops, people start coming from all over the neighborhood and the college. Some are still in their bathrobes. I'm there, too, of course, because I'm not about to sit and twiddle my thumbs where I was left off. The police are having a terrible time keeping everybody back. Seems like nobody in the crowd thinks about getting shot. Down below I see more police cars coming.

The police got the building surrounded and then I guess on account of Locke-Haven can't keep watch on every side, they manage to get into the front door and the back doors. An ambulance comes tearing up, and good thing too because another policeman gets shot in the shoulder and they're right there to lug him off.

Otto makes it into the front of the building with the police. Nobody's minding whether he's a policeman or not. The way I figure it they're mighty lucky he was with them. I get the details from him right after. Him and the police search the first floor, and the second floor, and they're creeping along on the third floor where they most suspect he's hiding. Otto's off to the side of the police, and he sees this little cranny and he sticks his head in, and there's a pistol sticking right in his forehead. He says he's been scared before but never like that. Then it comes to him that Harvey recognized him, otherwise he'd have been shot dead right there. So while he starts talking to Harvey he waves the police away with his hand behind him.

He says, Let me come in there, Harvey. I don't have a gun.

So Harvey lets him come in, and Otto calls to the police not to come anywheres near, and they promise they won't. Otto keeps on talking to him. This Harvey's all scrunched up, shaking and hungry, but so riled up he's ready to shoot anybody, even Otto maybe.

But Otto says to him, What good's it going to do? You killed one and shot three more. Why do you want to hurt anybody else? You're surrounded and can't get out.

Otto's got some Lifesavers that he was going to give to me but he gives them to Harvey instead and he's crunching at them like they're peanuts. Otto gets to talking to him about where they used to go swimming in the river and about high school days and about the war and about getting taken care of in a hospital, maybe even one away from Marchildon would be better so's he wouldn't have to think about Virgie.

Otto says, Boy, that was a mistake. I thought he was going to do me in right then, he got so mad.

Otto keeps trying to calm him down, and then the funny part is, they start to talking about me. This Locke-Haven asks Otto how come they knew where he was. He's sore on account of he was going to leave that night before the workmen come in the morning. So Otto tells him it was my idea.

You know what he said? Otto says. He says, That was Tom Mackie's boy on them handlebars. I'll be damned.

He's mad at first and then he laughs real hard and then he starts to cry. So Otto knows it's all over with, him just busting all to pieces crying. He gives up his gun and his bullets and comes out of the cranny with Otto. The police put handcuffs on him and bring him outside.

That's when I see him.

The crowd is getting bigger by then and starting to close in on him.

One guy says, Let us have him, Jake. Save you a lot of time and trouble.

Get out of the way, the chief says.

Who's going to feed Alice Preece's youngsters? one woman says, her mouth pulled back and big snaggly teeth sticking out.

Another guy says, Jud Preece was the best friend a man ever had.

Murderer, this ugly woman yells.

They're coming right at me, and the lane's getting closer all the time. Some grubby looking bum with glassy eyes and a rough beard lets go with a gob of spit and gets Harvey right in the face. He don't flinch.

That does it for me and I yells, Shut up, can't you see he's all tied up.

The people kind of stop pressing in. Harvey's eyes come up. He don't say anything to me. He just looks at me and his mouth twitches, but it isn't a mean twitch. A policeman's got sense to bring a patrol car up and it's driving right into the crowd, and before you know it Harvey's inside and being driven off.

I feel a hand on my shoulder. It's Otto and he looks all drained out.

Come on, Chip, let's go home, he says.

Ma isn't home from work yet and everybody's still asleep over at Otto's, so I invite him for breakfast. He takes me up on it, but first he goes over to get his Sunday paper. I fix us some eggs and toast and we have some Wheaties too, and we sit there and talk about Harvey being in the dormitory. Then we go out on the front porch to read the papers. He's got his in his chair and I got mine in mine. We sit there looking at the front page.

LOCKE-HAVEN AT LARGE sure isn't **LOCKE-HAVEN AT LARGE** anymore, I says.

Used to be yesterday's paper was old, but getting so even today's paper's old, he says.

We sit there reading all about the shooting. When I finish I look at the movies that are playing, but I don't see anything on that's any good, so I turn to the sports page. I'm reading about the Whiz Kids staying in first place, beating the Dodgers 6 to 4, Bob Miller winning his seventh straight and Jim Konstanty saving him, and about the Yankees dropping to third, and about Walt Dropo hitting a grand slammer for the Red Sox.

I hear Otto give a kind of groan behind his paper but he don't say anything. He's still in the front section, and I'm looking at the other headlines there on his front page that say **U.S. Troops Moving Up To Battlefront**, and little stuff, Red Korean columns outflank Suwon, and Americans head north from Taejon by truck toward combat zone, and 12 U.S. planes lost, and down at the bottom **Draft Plans Readied**.

Otto folds his paper and leans forward to point at a little box. He says, Read that, Chip, the first lines.

It says, Your day today, July 2, 1950. Today is the 183rd day of the year.

Know what that means? he says.

I says I don't.

Yesterday was 182 gone, and tomorrow is 182 to go. So what does today mean?

We're right in the middle, I says.

Chip, you are a scholar and a gentleman. We are in the middle, exactly in the middle day of the middle of the months in the middle of the year in the middle of the whole century. What do you make of that?

I don't know, except we're sure in the middle, I says.

He says, That we are. But you can't stay in the middle. I just wanted you to know where you are, like you've been on one side and now you swing on to the other, and you've got the whole rest of the century to find out what's going to happen.

I says, Well, if yesterday and today is a sign of what it's going to be like, I don't think it's going to be worth much.

We are still sitting there on the porch reading the papers when my mother come home.

THE RAKE'S PROGRESS

As young Professor Cooley settles deeper into his chair, trying with little success to immure himself from the voice of Eighteenth Century reading the paper on *Jonathan Wild*, he experiences a tightness in his throat, an unsettling throb in his rib cage. He looks out of Rickert Hall at the sunlight dancing on the plash of fountain in the quad. He has come to the college for the Saturday afternoon spring meeting of the Philological Association of the North Eight, or PANE, as it's called. The fountain, he was told, recovered only recently from the latest freshman prank. "Only the brand names change," one of the host members smiled. "They're always soggy, always empty." The testimony of well-heeled Sixties rebellion that lies this time under the usual mountain of suds is a giant-size box of Tide. To the left of the fountain, a horse chestnut tree burgeons tumescent pink blossoms. The brightness of the blue sky, the play of the water, and the madras modernity of the quad's brick and stone dazzle his eye. He swallows hard and rubs his rib cage and wonders at whatever can seize a man in such perfect health as he.

Thirty-two windows form the simulated Cantabrigian apse in which the speaker stands framed in an effulgence of light. Young Professor Cooley has counted them one by one: 14 full windows, 4 of them screened on each side, 18 half-size windows along the top. He fixes again upon Eighteenth Century: early thirties, black rimmed glasses, palmetto leaf of hair swept left, pipe bowl peeping out of his breast pocket like a diminutive periscope, weight already beginning to shift downward into his trousers, voice rising commensurately with his enthusiasm for Fielding:

" . . . as 'locked up in' in my explication of linked word-phrase motif in this dazzling and egregiously neglected masterpiece. Now 'lock up in,' 'lock out in,' and 'lock in out'—"

When Eighteenth Century turns the page, young Professor Cooley winces. PANE papers are supposed to last about thirty minutes. Young Professor Cooley, pretending to straighten his sleeve, steals a look at his wrist watch, sees that the paper has already gone a few minutes past the recommended limit, and estimates, by the sheets conspicuously in view, that half again as much remains. The first paper of the day, "A Re-evaluation of the Allegory of Time in *The Shepheardes Calender*," went at least a quarter of an hour overtime. Young Professor Cooley lost interest by April anyway. Now he sighs, which only intensifies the perturbation in his rib cage.

Propped against either side of the lectern are two gold-framed reproductions from Hogarth's *The Rake's Progress*. "Mr. Lloyd-Young told me that he brought these from his personal collection to titillate your senses in connection with aspects of sex, food, and drink in his paper on *Jonathan Wild*," the conference chairman said in his short introduction of the second speaker. The chuckle that accompanied his remark drew, in turn, understanding chuckles. It would have been hard to find a single member

of PANE, even among the some twenty-odd not in atten-
dance at this gathering, opposed to having his senses
titillated.

The glass covering the Fleet Prison scene on the left
catches the sunlight in such a way that young Professor
Cooley can see in its sheen a reflection of himself: Mark
Deiser Cooley, A.B., A.M., Ph.D., straight arrow, as
straight as the part of his hair which sits tight on his head
like a skullcap, face without wrinkle or scar, leather
patched sleeve on a three buttoner herringbone jacket over
button-down shirt and muted rep tie, to leave 32 behind on
the Sunday next for which he has no plans except to grade
a set of papers and prepare his lecture notes and work at his
article "Nymphs and Manias in Modern American Drama"
in his bachelor apartment with its racks of albums and its
rows of books and its silver-framed reproductions of
Chirico's *Era Moderna* and Feininger's *Church of the
Minorities* and his prized signed—though only a twelve-
dollar facsimile—*Christ of St John of the Cross*.

By moving his position, young Professor Cooley can
make out in the glass fuzzy reflections of some of the
dozen assorted faithful of PANE. Would they, he wonders,
during the polite quaffing of sherry at the conference
chairman's home, to which he's expected to accompany his
own department head, dare to say that *Jonathan Wild* is
hardly worth the trouble of resurrecting? Young Professor
Cooley believes it to be, save for a few mildly funny
moments, a fan waving in a void, a bad book, a dull book,
an insufferable book. No, decorum dictates otherwise. In
the get-together before the reading of the papers began, he
listened to the present speaker, like himself a second-year
assistant professor on trial, refer to Greene as "a feather-

weight" and Faulkner's work as "uhm-nonsensical opacity" without a murmur of dissent. What can one say to a man who carries a pipe, bowl up, in his pocket? Young Professor Cooley purses his mouth at the thought of the taste of an inverted stem—he carries his own pipe tucked in his belt, bowl down, and to the side, like an upside-down pistol.

The constriction remains in young Professor Cooley's throat. His rib cage throbs, as if there's something buried deep in his chest trying to get out. He puts on his glasses and looks outside again.

A young couple stands on the terrace above and beyond the fountain. He wonders how long they have been there: a boy whom he judges to be a sophomore, black haired, tanned as dark as an Indian brave, wearing a pale blue raglan sleeved shirt that hugs his upper biceps, and, bowed against him like a Siamese twin with whom he shares the same belly, a girl, perhaps also a sophomore, wearing a pink and white checkered summer dress, her wheat hair tied up in a bun, nearly as brown as the boy. Young Professor Cooley can see the flashing of the boy's teeth but can hear nothing except the voice of Eighteenth Century now on something to do with life in Newgate. And then young Professor Cooley blinks. The boy is kissing the girl. His hands move all over her back. Young Professor Cooley feels a prickly sensation along his scalp. He smoothes down his hair and lights up his pipe. A discreet cough comes from Seventeenth Century two armchairs away. Young Professor Cooley is beginning to perspire and, in spite of the little pot his middle makes, he opens his coat wide. The throb in his throat worsens and is now accompanied by a sweetish taste under his tongue.

Three small boys come whizzing past one by one on skateboards down the long sloping walk perpendicular to the steps from the terrace down to the level of the fountain. The skateboards muted by the closed windows in the apse make the sounds of zippers unzipping. The boys ignore the young lovers. The college boy, bent to yet another kiss, continues to fondle the girl's back, oblivious of the three interlopers.

At the appearance of the three boys on their skateboards, two azure birds, which young Professor Cooley has not previously seen, burst from the horse chestnut tree into the quad area and disappear in cardiographic lines of flight against the buildings. He does not know what kind of birds they are.

"And sex figures oh quite prominently," Eighteenth Century says, "in the marvelous scene at sea when Mrs. Heartfree is accosted by Wild and rejected him 'with all the repulses which indignation and horror could animate. But when he attempted violence, she filled the cabin with her shrieks, which were so vehement that they reached the ears of the captain, the storm at this time luckily abating. This man, who was a brute, rather from his education, and the element he inhabited, than from nature, ran hastily down to her assistance, and finding her struggling on the ground [*sic*, young Professor Cooley thinks] with our hero, he presently rescued her from her intended ravisher; who was soon obliged to quit the woman, in order to engage with her lusty champion, who spared neither pains nor blows in the assistance of his said passenger. When the short battle was over, in which our hero, had he not been overpowered with numbers, who came down on their captain's side, would have been victorious; the captain rapped out a hearty oath, and asked Wild, If he had no more Christianity in him than to ravish a woman in a storm!'" The PANE members chuckle in a body. A smile as full of delight as a Halloween pumpkin's spreads over the face of Eighteenth Century. He waits, then resumes: "Now, as you see, when we re-examine the paradigm of the—"

Young Professor Cooley makes a mental note to cut from the paper that he's to read at the next meeting of PANE the scene from *The Hamlet* in which the school-teacher Labove attempts to rape Eula. Young Professor Cooley might not have agreed to present his paper had it not been for certain prompting by his department head, P. Dominy Quint, who takes a zealous interest, academic and otherwise, in the activities of his staff. But it is on publication that he whets his saber, and nearly every time that he sees young Professor Cooley of late he asks him for the latest progress report on his dissertation, *The Sex Goddess in Contemporary Literature*, which, having gone through three revisions, is now being considered by one of the university presses. After all, young Professor Cooley's name has yet to appear on one of the bi-monthly summaries of publication by department members (referred to by the staff simply as the PorP sheet) on which there is always appended next to the florid initials PDQ such exhortations as "Good show, boys—keep it up" and "Let's all go over the top next time, boys." And *boys* literally, young Professor Cooley thinks, for there are no women on the staff. "Hire one of them and first thing they got a baby," old Professor Quint says, assuming his Bantam rooster stance.

Young Professor Cooley blinks again. Three young coeds in bikini bathing suits of varying fuchsia shades come by the fountain, unaware of the group seated inside the hall. They sit down on the edge of the fountain and spin around. Young Professor Cooley's buttocks tighten. The girls dunk their feet into the fountain pool. He can hear the faint strains of a pulsating musical beat to which one girl snaps her fingers and bobs her head and shoulders. The loreleis do not stay there long before picking up their towels and their transistor radio and their beach bags and ambling into the quad area toward one of the dormitories. They ignore the young boys, who have momentarily abandoned their skateboards for a heads-together consultation over candy bars on a grassy slope, but cast sidelong glances at the lovers nose to nose above them.

" . . . juxtaposed to the character of Laetitia Snap. And you'll recall Mrs. Heartfree's speech, 'How shall I describe the tumult of passions which then laboured in my breast.' In a recent number of *Literature and Psychology*, dated—"

Young Professor Cooley sucks on his pipe and finds that it has gone out. For a moment the young lovers are lost from his view. The two azure birds alight in the tree again and disappear behind its bulbously erect blossoms. Then the boy and girl reappear at the fountain as Eighteenth Century is bending over to explain the iconography of the Hogarth tavern scene on the right.

"You see, while the hussy in the right foreground here is undressing, the one over here has removed the watch from our prodigal's pocket, and it's being passed back to this—"

Chuckles come from the semicircle of the PANE audience lopsided to the left. Although they are looking toward the painting, it's difficult to tell whether they are chuckling at it or at the lovers by the fountain. However, young Professor Cooley can see that most of the PANE group is disadvantageously seated to observe the latter. The delighted pumpkin smile is back again on Eighteenth Century's face.

The sunlight dazzles and the water plashes and the horse chestnut tree throbs with life. The boy bends the girl backward, eyes closing, and kisses her, a long exploratory kiss, and undoes the bun of her hair. The mane of her hair falls into the fountain's pool, but she remains motionless in his embrace.

Young Professor Cooley wonders what the boy will do if he happens to look up and to see that he's being watched. He must see, young Professor Cooley thinks as he stares at the boy's bent head. He will flush to the roots of his hair and hide his eyes and turn his face and slink away.

The girl, turned partially away from the windows, now has her head over the boy's shoulder. He holds the weight of her sopping mane up from the water. And the boy is looking directly into young Professor Cooley's face from not more than perhaps thirty feet away. He is saying something to the girl, her face now in profile, and looking straight at young Professor Cooley. Then he is wrapping her hair about her, and her head is thrown back in laughter.

His eyes still on young Professor Cooley, the boy takes out a package of gum and puts a stick in his mouth. He chews it slowly, easily, the jaw muscles working rhythmically over the gum, and leans forward to kiss the girl, and then she is chewing the gum and laughing. And the boy smiles at young Professor Cooley and takes out another stick of gum and begins to chew on it slowly. Then as they stand faced away from the windows, she close at his side, he takes the girl's pony tail in his hand, holds it slung about the back of his neck, and they walk away, arms around each other's waists. The fountain plashes gaily. The tree is bursting with vivid color.

Young Professor Cooley's face is flushed. With his hand over his lowered eyes, he glances at his watch: 3 o'clock. Eighteenth Century, even though just reporting that Wild was taken from Newgate to Tyburn and hanged there on Monday, May 25, 1725, has lost none of his enthusiasm, and the paper is moving into its second hour. Young Professor Cooley's heart pounds, his throat is dry, and the taste below his tongue has become an intense but inexplicable craving.

Young Professor Cooley knows suddenly that he cannot make it. He knows that he has to escape, he *must* escape. He's going to rise from his chair, a sneer on his lips, draw all eyes, Eighteenth Century's in particular, to him, and walk out, out into the open sunshine, boldly, proudly, chest up and back straight.

He takes off his glasses and looks to his left. Middle Ages' chair blocks the only egress. On the right, Nineteenth Century gives him a blurred smile from beneath her bird-nest hat. There is room between her chair and that of the conference chairman, just enough room to squeeze through. Young Professor Cooley leans forward.

"Irwin himself writ small when he said that here Fielding writ small. On the contrary, we should look to Digeon who wrote, 'It probes down deep into our soul,' and Wendt who maintained in his 'The Moral Allegory of *Jonathan Wild*'—"

Young Professor Cooley sees himself walking out to revel in the sunlight, the freshness of the air, the beauty of the trees. He will wink at the first pretty girl who passes him by. Maybe he will even put his feet in the fountain. He buttons his coat, he taps out his pipe, he smoothes down his hair, and moves farther forward in his chair until his weight is on the balls of his feet.

Eighteenth Century turns another page. Young Professor Cooley sits poised at the edge of his chair. He stares into the empty fireplace that he can see blurry in the space between the two chairs on his right. He puts his glasses back on. The marble exterior of the fireplace gleams. The brick base on the inside has been scrubbed clean. The gleaming andiron is empty. Young Professor Cooley glances at the lectern. He sees that there are only two or maybe three pages left at most. Slowly he begins to move backward into his chair. His heart flutters and slows to a dull hollow throbbing. Then he sits back all the way in his chair as immobile as a petrified tree.

Polite applause sounds and young Professor Cooley sees that the paper has gone four minutes over an hour and he begins tapping his hands together without sound and he is sweating and his ears are ringing and his brain feels ossified, like a lump of putty left too long out-of-doors. Middle Ages smiles cheerily beside him and says, "Devastating, wasn't it?" And young Professor Cooley is getting up, and he knows as he stands there, stretching, arms wide, head pulled back by a crick deep in his neck, the hollow like an abyss inside his chest, that he has experienced some irredeemable loss, but for all his degrees and all his critical acumen and all his finely tuned sensibilities he does not know what it is.

SANS EVERYTHING

Idiot, Bonner mutters under her breath as she follows Leola into a small dark room off the back hallway where Leola's mother lies propped up in a high narrow bed. Although Bonner won't admit it in public, she dislikes old people, in particular women who allow age to warp their beauty, dim their senses, or sap their vitality. They're better off dead.

Leola smiles down. "She's come, Mama. This is Bonner Adams Meyering, my friend, that wrote the book."

"He is?" the old woman squawks. Her toothless, nearly bald head lifts a fraction off the pillow, and she tries to focus her cataractal eyes. Her beads have fallen from the bed, and Leola bends to pick them up.

Bonner's nose flares at the smell of Wizard Spring Bouquet spray deodorizer in the room. On one wall hangs a tarnished crucifix, on another a large and fading pietà in a chipped black frame. On a table beside the bed, like a miniature nativity scene, are a dozen or so figurines. The paint has worn off them, and Bonner can't tell what they're supposed to represent. On the other side of the bed in a dome shaped, bronze barred cage sleeps a parakeet, so fat and so still that it might be stuffed.

"Gabby's kept her company for ages," Leola says. "Mama, listen to me, she's here, my friend, Bonner Adams Meyering."

When Bonner steps forward to extend her hand, she kicks a bedpan. The old woman's hand is as light and bony as a bird claw, with veins running like teal ropes along the forearm. Goose bumps spring up on Bonner's arm.

The old woman tilts up her chin, and her high thin voice quavers. "Oh, such a fine young woman for you, son. But, remember, son, don't molest her."

Leola clucks. "She's got worse and worse lately." Her hands are cupped over the beads as if she has trapped an Easter chick eager to pop out and scurry away. "Mama, you wanted to tell her about Orville. Mama, she came all this way. Oh Mama."

Light swims up out of the old woman's chlorinated eyes for an instant. Gripping Bonner's thumb, she tries to pull her closer. Bonner bends toward the hemstitched mouth. "Why is Daughter so mean to me? Daughter makes me take all those uggh." A disdainful flutter of her moss-veined lids takes in the rows of bottles and jars and boxes on a dresser top. She pulls Bonner closer. She smells like a dried washcloth. "Get rid of her. I can't stand her anymore."

The old woman's head sinks back on the pillow. Leola places the beads on her breast. The links catch the light like tiny diamonds in a chunk of slag. When the old woman moves, the beads slide serpentine down along her side.

"Now remember, son, don't molest her." The old woman's eyes close. As Bonner heads out the door she hears the old woman say, "Is that you, Orville?" Bonner peers backward and aslant. The only part of the old woman that sticks up from the bed are her feet. Leola closes the door and says, "I'm so sorry."

"Who's Orville?" Bonner says.

"That's what it was she wanted to tell you about."

Leola edges sideways toward the living room, hands clasping her forearms, eyes lowered. Jesus-Lord-God, a regular Sissy Meek, Bonner grumbles to herself, recalling the nickname whispered behind the back of a nun by the older kids and even by other brawnier sisters at the Catholic school she attended as a child. Nobody, but nobody, like that ever inherited the earth. Everything about Leola annoyed Bonner: her shyness, her soft voice, the horsy face shorn of make-up, the hair that screams for a hairdresser, the flat chested, hipless figure, the cotton dress blotched by bouquets of violets. Bonner is convinced that she can be taken for Leola's daughter, which, considering that they're both thirty-seven, gives her much satisfaction. Yet at the same time the difference between them rubs her the wrong way. There's no reason for a woman to go downhill when—to use one of her favorite expressions—it's so easy to ooze sex appeal. She asks again who Orville is.

"My brother."

"I didn't know you have a brother."

"I didn't know him. I was only two when he died."

"What does she want to tell me?"

"How he died."

"Well, how *did* he die?"

"He was lynched."

"Lynched?"

"Yes, right here in San Adelphi. Thirty-five years ago. That was before we moved to Idaho."

"What do you mean he was lynched. White men don't get lynched. And in California?—I never heard of such a thing."

"Well, he was. And he was only sixteen and a half years old." Leola's hands are still clasping her forearms which she keeps pressed against her body.

Bonner selects what seems the best chair in the Montgomery Ward ensemble of Early American furniture. A lump pokes against her backside, and she readjusts her position. She sits facing the blank eye of a bulky television set. Her mouth purses when she checks the trademark. Maybe Leola isn't very well fixed, but there's no reason to put up with an old junky model in this day and age of credit cards.

Leola sits at the edge of her seat, legs together to one side. "I'm so glad you're going to stay for a minute. You so busy with your book and all. Are you sure you won't have some coffee or something?"

"Are you going to tell me about your brother now or not?"

Leola hesitates. "It all started over one of the Lord girls. You'd have thought she'd be real high-tone, I mean, the Lords ran the whole county."

"Lord?"

"Yes, the department store right where you were today. The very same. He's dead now, the old man, Mr. Lord. Cancer. His sons own it now, a whole big chain. Anyway his daughter ran away with a buyer and got married and Mr. Lord, he got mad as the dickens and went and had it annulled. So she came back to town. She was a"—she makes a *tsk*—"you know, a wild girl. Mama says she used to walk down the street the jiggly way she did just to get the boys to watch. All decked out, fit to kill, well, I didn't mean it that way, I mean, Harry, I guess he was the one that started it. He was older than Orville, thirty-something, I expect. Like I told you, Orville, he was just sixteen and a half. You know what's bound to happen." She stops as if expecting a reply.

"No, I don't," Bonner says.

"Copycatting him. Orville started to copycat him, tagging after him, doing everything he did. Who could have told? Orville, when he was littler, when Papa was still home, he was an altar boy, never missed church, even told Mama once he wanted to be a priest. Well, one night this Harry got drunk, and got Orville to take some whiskey too. They saw this Lord girl and, next thing, she was in the car with them. She got in all by herself—they didn't force her or anything like that. They took her out in the country, and she got to teasing Harry. He was the kind had a mean streak in him. He hit her, then he must have gone crazy. He raped her and beat her up real bad. Nobody knows exactly what happened, whether she was lying or Orville lied because he told Mama he never even touched her, all he did was drive. The girl said both of them raped her. She said it was Orville pushed her out of the car. He told Mama he was driving and Harry was in the back seat with the girl on the way back to town. She got pushed out or jumped or fell out. Whatever it was, Harry made Orville keep on going. Somebody saw the girl on the road and brought her into town. She told all about Harry and Orville before she died."

Leola begins to chew her lip.

A twinge darts in and out of Bonner's pelvis, and she doesn't know why. She shifts her position.

Leola lets out a long breath. "So they came and got Orville and put him in jail with Harry. Mama went to see Orville that day, and that was the last time, because that night all these people started coming to the jail. Mama says there were thousands of them, maybe five thousand. They got a telephone pole, and they battered down the jail doors, all like they went crazy. The sheriff and the deputies just stood there. They said later they got knocked out and tied up, which wasn't true at all. Anyways, all these people got

Orville and Harry outside and tore off all their clothes and hung them up on an elm tree right there in the street. It was real bad. They didn't just hang them. They whipped them and cut them and—I can't tell you what all they did, you'd get sick."

Bonner stares at Leola.

Leola sits back as if surprised that she has spoken at such length. She sighs and clears her throat. "They killed the tree, carving their names, signing I was here. Lots of people came for souvenirs—they ripped off bark, they tore off limbs. So it's gone now, the tree. The old jail isn't there anymore either. Everything's changed, new stores all around, like the new building Lord's is in, and a big new hotel right across the street."

"The Mirador? That's where I am."

Leola does not seem to hear. "First thing we did when we moved back here from Idaho Falls—it's been three years now—was to go look at the place. Mama sort of gave a little cry and said, 'Everything's gone.' She's been in bed since. Not quite right anymore, like you saw. I guess that was the last lynching here, I don't know, maybe there'll be another one sometime. But they don't remember it at all here. Like it never happened. Sure happened to Mama, though: her going to get him, looking up from the bottom of that tree, seeing him hanging there, what was left of him."

Bonner shudders. "What did she want to tell me a thing like that for?"

"Because you write in books."

"But my book, it's not about—my goodness." Bonner sits back in her chair. What did a story of such grotesque violence have to do with her? The old woman is obviously senile, so no logical reason exists for summoning Bonner to hear about Orville. It's all crazy. Yet a curious tugging at the back of her mind signals some connection between the story and her book. Riddles annoy her. She can't comprehend this one, nor does she even want to think about it.

Bonner is beginning to soften toward Leola. Not that she likes her any better, but she does feel a little sorry for her. "I don't see how you can stand to live in this place."

"Mama wanted to be with Orville. Funny thing is, he's not even buried in San Adelphi. They wouldn't put him in the cemetery. He's in a little town about thirty miles away. Course it doesn't bother me—my name isn't the same."

Bonner seizes on the change of subject to rid her mind of the old woman. "What happened to your husband?"

Leola winces and murmurs that she had raised her two daughters by herself since they were small. Under Bonner's persistent questioning, she admits that her husband ran off with another woman. "She was in cosmetics in Kirk Drug. You remember Kirk Drug, don't you? That was where all the kids used to go for cokes after school. I sat next to you one time when you were having a cherry coke with Irma and Gwendolyn Lacy. You even talked to me. You said to the fountain boy, 'Heavy on the cherry, Larry.' His name was Newell. I laughed so hard I like to died. Everything you said was so funny. Do you remember?"

Bonner doesn't remember, but she continues to say "Oh yes" here and "Oh yes" there to mention of names and classes and events, all as hazy as her recollection of the girl who became this homely, careworn woman. The lynching incident stays naggingly in the back of her mind.

"Are your mother and father still back in Idaho Falls?"

"I haven't seen them for years," Bonner says. "I can't stand the place."

"In the paper it said you were—uhh, I thought you were married."

"I was once, back in Salt Lake. It didn't work out."
Bonner breathes a long stream of smoke, and admires the
band of tiny diamonds set in her cigarette holder. "What I
wanted wasn't what he wanted: tract house, kids, PTA,
crabgrass, recipe cards. Besides, he wasn't any good in
bed. I cut out and headed for LA. Started out copywriting
in radio. Got my big break in an ad agency. Didn't take me
long to find out all a girl's got to do is stay on the ball,
play politics, sleep around in the right places." Her
conspiratorial wink is intended to convince Leola that the
facts are otherwise. When Leola gives her a blank stare,
Bonner adds, "Don't worry, I never felt a thing. No, what
did it was they gave me a little cosmetics account. I revised
their whole ad approach, right from scratch. Heavy on sex
appeal. In two years I tripled their profits. From then on it
was gravy. All the best accounts. Took me just from '56 to
'63. Same hype: sex, sex, sex. Toss in glops of love and
romance to satisfy the sentimentalists. Don't think I still
don't work like a bastard. I cleared seventy thousand last
year. Now my book, and it's going like a skyrocket."

Leola looks at her wide eyed. In turn Bonner surveys
her critically. "Maybe your husband wouldn't have left you
if—look, why don't you do something with yourself. My
first years in LA I got my nose fixed, teeth capped, breasts
lifted. You'd be surprised what things like that can do for
you."

"I couldn't do anything like that."

"O come on, Leola. Don't be a lump. How do you
think I keep my complexion? How do you think I stay a
size 9? Because I work like hell at it, that's why. Read
about my system of Sexercise, my Calory Cross plan, my
posetures, and you'll find out. Do you ever go out?"

"Well, there are the girls, and then Mama—somebody
has to take care of her."

86   *Sans Everything*

"And who takes care of you?"

"I go out. I—I go to church. Father Twitchell says—"

"Jesus-Lord-God, woman. You want a man, don't you? We outnumber them, for pity sakes, so a woman's got to do everything possible to make herself sexy and alluring." Bonner points toward her book, which lies under Leola's purse on the coffee table. The sales slip is still poking out from the pages. "Wisest thing you ever did was spend that $13.95. You'll learn how to improve yourself, give yourself some style, master the come-ons. Have a look at the epitaph I wrote. Go on, read it, right there at the front."

"I don't know what that is, epitaph."

"It's a little poem I wrote for the beginning of the book. Here."

Leola reads in a breathy monotone:

SEX

SEX   SEX

makes

everything

whole.

B.A.M.

"Doesn't that charge you up?" Bonner says. "You read that book, every line, it's a sincere book."

"Oh Bonnie, I know it's a sincere book and all, but—"

The door flies open, which spares Bonner from responding to a name she hasn't heard for twenty years.

A girl of about fourteen bounces in, drops an armful of books on a chair, and heads for the television set. The screen burgeons pointy breasted girls with swinging manes of hair gyrating to the screeches of mop haired boys slapping at long guitars that extend out of their crotches. The girl begins to sway, throws her head from side to side, snaps her fingers. Another girl, perhaps a year older, slouches in, makes a face at the first one, and heads for the refrigerator.

"Children—"

The guitar twanging and the adenoidal wail from the TV remains at a loud volume as the girls are introduced to Bonner. Gloria Jean slurps a dish of canned pears, and Doralee looks out of the corner of her eye at the TV.

Over a break from the music can be heard the feeble voice of the old woman from the back bedroom.

Leola starts away, stops, squeezes her forearms into her body, and looks from Bonner to her daughters. "Why don't you go see what Gramma wants?"

Doralee screws up her face and makes no move away from the TV set. Leola turns to the other girl who is now peeling a banana. "Oh, what does she want anyway?"

"Gloria Jean!"

"It's all right," Bonner says. "You go ahead. The girls can take care of me." She watches the MC who is manipulating two puppets, one with long blonde hair and the other with dark hair in bangs down to its eyes, and speaking in falsetto voice on how to "avoid bad breath and be kissin' sweet." She met him once and liked him. Thanks to cosmetic surgery, he actually looked 22 at 42. "He's something, isn't he?" Bonner says.

"He's okay," Doralee says.

"He's a jerk," Gloria Jean says.

"I'll bet you like the music."

Gloria Jean makes another face.

"Them—they make me sick," Doralee says.

"Why do you watch it, then?"

Neither one answers. Bonner hears a toilet flushing.

The youngest girl picks up the book on the coffee table and when she turns it over and sees the front of the jacket she puts her hand over her mouth, chin cupped in her palm and her fingers forming a cone over her nose. Her sister rushes over and goes through the same motions. Doralee rubs a finger at her mother, who is just returning, and says, "Mama, shame on you." They keep their hands over their mouths.

Leola reddens, which means that she is either embarrassed for herself or for her guest—Bonner can't tell. In either case she wants to take Leola by the shoulders and shake her until her teeth rattle. Leola is probably the kind of mother who never utters an obscenity, let alone the word *sex*. In the preface of her book Bonner roasts all those finger-wagging types who cluck "naughty-naughty" at their precious little tykes whenever the subject of sex comes up.

"I'm so sorry," Leola says, grimacing. "They're only children."

Bonner looks at Gloria Jean's breasts straining against her T-shirt. Wait until the kids get to Chapter III, "How To Get It If You Haven't Got It," or Chapter VIII, "Six Days To Multiple Orgasms," or Chapter XII, "How To Handle Your Affairs."

Leola takes the book from Doralee. "Don't you see the name here? Bonner wrote this book, it's a best-seller."

The girls stare at Bonner.

"No kidding," one says.

"Cross my heart," Bonner says.

"Jeez," says the other.

"Bonner is one of the most famous authors in America today," Leola says. "We went to school together in Idaho."

While the girls listen to their mother, Bonner sees again in the surging crowd at Lord's the lump out of the sagebrush past. Book clutched to her bosom, lines rehearsed, she still struggled to express her mission, a mission in itself so odd that it somehow moved Bonner to comply.

"Yes, she was downtown this afternoon autographing copies. See, here's where she signed. See where she wrote, 'To My Old And Dear Friend.'"

"It looks like it says Leora," Gloria Jean says.

"I make a weird *l*, sweetie," Bonner says.

"We study authors in school and all, but they never seem like real people, I mean like they're alive or anything," Doralee says.

Bonner laughs.

The MC disappears into a point of light, and the girls are at Bonner's feet. Their questions are no more and no less inane than the ones usually asked by her admirers. Even though such adulation is—as she always says—*quelle bore*, she is nevertheless annoyed when a quarter of an hour later the girls begin to stir. Gloria Jean gets up to check the time and announces upon her return, "Mama, we still want to go swimming."

Doralee jumps up. "You promised, Mama. It's after four o'clock. You promised."

"But, children, Bonner's here. We were having such a nice talk."

"Oh," the girls respond in unison.

"Think of everything you'll have to tell your friends," Leola says.

"I've got to go anyway." Bonner rises.

"Oh, I wish you could stay, but you so busy and all. I'll take you back to town."

Another feeble cry comes from the bedroom.

"Go ahead and get ready, girls," Leola says.

While Leola is taking care of her mother, Gloria Jean comes out and asks Bonner to zip up the back of her swim suit. She gazes down at the illustration of a sun-bronzed, bikini-clad girl on the book jacket, over which is superimposed the title in white letters. "Wouldn't it be neat to have one like that?"

Bonner studies the girl's surprisingly well-formed hips. "You must have a yummy boyfriend."

"Naw."

"I bet all the boys think you're a terrific little sexpot."

"Not in this cruddy old thing."

The girl is right—the suit looks like a green pepper with ruffles. Bonner tugs at the zipper. To get it straight, she puts her hand on the girl's backside. The flesh is solid, moistly hot under her palm. She feels a twinge deep in her loin, tiny, like a diamond giving off glints of light. She works the zipper up a few teeth at a time and smoothes out the seam with meticulous care along the small of the back. "That's quite a roller coaster you've got. Zoop, down it goes like this, and—"

Doralee comes into the room. Bonner takes her hand away and zips up the zipper the rest of the way. "You, too," she says. "All rightee, turn around."

Upon her return, Leola addresses the floor. "One of you girls will have to stay. Gramma is not feeling good."

"No, you promised," Doralee says.

"She can stay by herself," Gloria Jean says. "She's not a baby."

Leola winces at Bonner. "Poor thing, she's got terrible gas."

Bonner winces too. "I tell you what, why don't you call me a cab. I can drop the girls off at the pool on the way. Then you won't have to leave the house. Go on, girls, get something on over those suits."

"A cab?" Doralee says.

"It would be imposing," Leola says

"Nonsense," Bonner says.

"Somebody there will have a car," Gloria Jean says. "We can get a ride back."

"Sure," Bonner says.

Leola chews at the corner of her lip. "Well-l, the rec center is right near. And I did promise them."

"It's settled then," Bonner says.

At the sidewalk Leola kisses Bonner on the cheek. "I just can't thank you enough for coming. I'm sorry it turned out like this, with Mama—"

"Stop apologizing," Bonner says. "You do what I told you. You study that book of mine like it was the Bible, and the men'll be tearing down your door."

"I'll try," Leola says.

The two girls, flanking Bonner in the seat, wave to their mother through the rear window. Bonner gives the destination to the driver.

"Lord's?" Doralee turns. "You said you were going to take us to the pool."

"You'll get there, don't worry. I have to make a little stop first." Bonner sits back, folds her arms, and smiles. She likes having the girls beside her. She has rarely been around children and is surprised by the pleasant glow she feels.

Doralee leans forward and points. "That's where we go to church. It's the Holy Cross Methodist."

Bonner expresses surprise that they don't belong to the same church as their mother and grandmother.

"Daddy didn't want us to."

"Church is dumb," Gloria Jean says. "Who wants to sit there and listen to all that cruddy old stuff you can't understand."

"What church do you go to?" Doralee asks.

"I don't, honey."

"Why not?"

"You don't have to go to church to be religious," Bonner replies.

At a curve the taxi appears to be headed directly into a billboard depicting a majestic white automobile draped in jewelry against a powder blue background. The girls are paying no attention to the route. Bonner can feel their eyes on her.

"How d'you get your complexion so beautiful?" Gloria Jean asks.

"The most important thing for you is to eat the right food. And no dark liquids to drink either."

"Aw, we know all that. We want to know about make-up."

"How do you get your eyes like that? your mouth?" Doralee asks. "Mama won't let me use any lipstick."

"Oh a little touch won't hurt you." Bonner leans toward her face. "Probably light pink. Some make-up would cover these blemishes."

Doralee blushes.

"That's all right, honey. If you want to know, I had the world's worst case of acne when I was your age."

"You did?"

"Yes I did."

"She picks her face," Gloria Jean says.

"We're going to have to do something about that nose of yours, aren't we?"

Gloria Jean blushes.

"Nothing could help that beak," Doralee says.

"I'll fix you," Gloria Jean says.

"You'd be surprised what darker make-up can do," Bonner says. "Right down the center would help it. Now, your face is a bit round, so you'll want to apply some in the cheeks, you see, yes, there in the hollows. Sneak a peek at 'Making Out With Make-up' in my book. When you're all fresh and shiny the boys'll be falling out of the trees after you."

The girls giggle. The taxi pulls up in front of Lord's.

"Isn't it fabulous?" Doralee says. "It's the biggest store in San Adelphi."

"We come down here sometimes and spend the whole day just looking at things."

"And they got parking way down underground. My girlfriend's boyfriend—he's got this neat car; they've been going steady for two years—he took us down one time, round and round, all the way to the bottom."

Bronzed doors spring open at their footsteps upon wine carpeting that extends to the sidewalk. Panel-sculptured on each door are modernistic designs of a refrigerator, stove, dishwasher, vanity table, bathing suit, necklace, and fur coat. They pass banks of television sets, all flashing the same picture of a scantily clad, bronzed woman lying on a tiger rug and dabbing her neck with perfume.

"Mine," Bonner says at the commercial.

Sofas, armchairs with hassocks, and recliner chairs face the television sets in rows as orderly as pews. Side by side along a stained glass wall beyond are room groupings of furniture: Italian provincial, Spanish provincial, French provincial. Each dining room table displays a different centerpiece of artificial pastel flowers and varicolored candles swirling up out of bronze, brass, and sterling silver candelabras.

The sprightly strains of "Get Me To The Church On Time" waft over the aisles.

They bypass a small crowd around a collection of mirrors in all sizes and shapes. Signs in the mirrors read √Super Easter Special! and »Once-in-a-Lifetime Price!! and > > >Easterrific Salerama!!!

She leads the girls to the booknook at the head of the aisle. They fall quiet before a large white-lettered sign on a tripod: **BONNER ADAMS MEYERING**, in person, noon to 3 p.m. Another sign to the right reads: ♥High Priestess of Sex. A third to the left reads: 'The new sexual manifesto: look sexy, act sexy, be sexy.' Printed in purple letters on a large, gold, star-shaped sign hanging above:

The Year's

Blazing

Blockbuster

Copies of Bonner's book fill racks on three sides. The brilliant crimson of the book jackets matches the background color of the floor signs. Above the books float red balloons bearing in white various trinities:

SEX	S S S	S
SEX SEX	EEE	EEE
SEX SEX SEX	X	X X X

On the back wall of the booknook next to a decorative artificial tree hangs a portrait of Bonner in a baby spotlight. The girls gape upward. Bonner eyes it with the same pleasure she had twelve cities back when the tour began: the wide intelligent forehead, the shadowy high cheekbones, the brows arched just so—Pandor must have taken at least thirty poses to get that arch—the sensual pouting underlip, the triangular cut of the chin, the hair in a casual flip, the swell of the bust below pearl choker.

Beyond a few women circling an obelisk stack of her book she sees her promotion agent. She frowns. "Go wander around for a bit, girls."

"How'd it go, sweetheart?" he says. He's a dashingly handsome young man, with black hair and swarthy skin, but there's something askew about his face. His white even teeth are too plentiful and large for the size of the mouth, and the nose, straight and pointed, is too small for the size of the cheeks.

"You're supposed to be in San Jose," Bonner says.

"I'm on my way. Well, do I give it the big play or not? Answering appeal of sick old woman et cetera, et cetera."

"Next time you get a brainstorm, keep it to yourself."

"It was your idea as much as mine. What are you doing with the two chicks? That one looks ripe enough to pluck."

"You get your can in gear and get to San Jose. If you don't do better than what you did here, Van Dine is going to hear from me."

"You got everything they got here: one newspaper, one channel, the radio stations. What do you want anyway?"

"You know what I want."

"You just leave it up to old Lance boy, sweetheart. The schedule's going to be tight tomorrow. I mean real saturation. You'll be at it all day and half the night."

"I'll leave you in the dust, Hymie boy."

He blinks. "Please don't call me that."

"Where did you steal Lance Larabee anyway?" She stops smiling. "Now get, Hymie boy."

She watches the rigidly braced shoulders of the Brooks Brothers suit move away. She has to hurt him, not because she wants to, but because he's so obnoxious. He has no class and deserves what he gets.

From among the teased hair, designer slacks, and sunsensor glasses in the booknook comes a wide hipped woman bearing a copy of the book, pen poised.

"You're her."

"I'm her."

Bonner scrawls her name inside the cover, the first letters of each name very large and the rest almost indecipherable, except for the low sweeping *y*'s at the last.

The woman bends to her ear. "It's for my girlfriend at McConkey Plumbing, not me."

Bonner looks at the tiny blood vessels in the woman's nostrils. "Of course. What's your girlfriend's name?"

"Uh, Olga."

Above her name, Bonner writes *For Olga* and hands the book back.

The woman's face falls.

Bonner backs away. It's past 4:30. Can't they read? She wishes the girls would come back. She feels like a piece of sales goods. Another comes, a mole boring in: thick glasses, a mustache of sandy down, and an eroded chin.

"I'm from Philomela Club, Mrs. Meyering—it's a book club. I'm giving a report. I read the critics, and some of them, boy, they sure worked you over. On that talk show the other day you said the world would be a better place when we learn to act out all our sexual fantasies, boy, that minister, she sure let you have it."

Bonner stares at her. She hates these women—no, she loves them. She does, she's trying to help them, to bring them into the new age. Can't they see that? Why can't they leave her alone? But she has asked for all this, wants it, drives for it. She feels a moment of panic. Why is she feeling at raw edge? Twelve cities and this has never happened. Why can't they like her? She's likable, wants to be liked. Many do—they love her, they pull at her clothes, they hang on her arm. But what about these few, always snapping at her heels? She will not lose her temper, no, that she'll never do. Bonner stretches her mouth into what she calls her frozen she-wolf smile. She can stay in it for three hours straight.

"Lots of critics didn't like *Moby Dick* when it was published, or *Ulysses*," Bonner says.

"You're not comparing your book to *them*?"

"Did I do that? All I said was, critics didn't like those books either. Of course my book isn't *that* kind of classic. But you check the sales charts. Only two books had bigger first printings in the past five years: *The Naked Countess* and *How To Get Rich Without Working*. Mine's tops so far for this year. That's nothing to sneeze at, is it? You be sure and tell that to all your Philodendron girlfriends, won't you?"

"It's not—"

"You must forgive me, dear, but I have to run."

Bonner finds the two girls laughing over contemporary Easter cards at a notions counter. She leads them to the elevator where she studies the store directory for a moment. She punches 3, smiles at the girls, and hums along to the elevator's strains of "Invitation."

"Where are we going anyway?" Gloria Jean says.

"This is the place, girls." Bonner leads them to the swim wear department. "You said you liked the bathing suit on the cover of my book. I want you to have one like it. You too, sweetie. On me."

The girls draw in their breath and clap their hands to their cheeks.

"Well, get to it. Pick out the prettiest ones you can find. They have to be right for you, though."

A salesgirl who looks familiar to Bonner comes to assist. She pays little attention to the girls and keeps smiling hugely at Bonner.

"Yes, they're all right . . . for Idaho Falls," Bonner says of the suits that the salesgirl first shows them. "Now, what do you have for the Riviera?"

When the girls have picked out two suits and withdraw to try them on, the salesgirl descends upon Bonner from around the counter. She's platinum haired and hollow cheeked and wears green eye shadow.

"Can I talk to you for a sec, Miss Meyering? You autographed my book I bought at lunch—I was the next to the first one. I was first till that fat slob shoved herself in front of me. I spent my whole lunch hour reading. I didn't even eat because I couldn't hardly put it down." She glances over her shoulder. "Just between you and I, I got it open under there, and when nobody's looking, I . . . you know what I mean. It's like a miracle, your coming up here. Do you know what I mean, like when you keep thinking and thinking about something, and then it goes and happens, just like a miracle."

"Well, I'm glad you like the book," Bonner says, backed against the counter.

"Like it?—are you kidding? I'm crazy about it. Everything you say is so true, so absolutely for-real true. I mean about not having to be married and still have sex all over and about what to do when you're lovers with a married man, and oh, like how to entice men, like you said a ski lodge. Last Christmas at Tahoe I met three different boys. One of them even started to teach me how to ski, and like—oh, the best part, your Ten Commandments on being sexy, Thou shalt like men, and Thou shalt love sex, and Thou—well, Judas Priest, everyone of them fits me to a T, like about flirting and about having organisms every time and about making the upmost of your face and body, whatever typical type you happen to be. See, beings as I'm willowy—that's what this college boy told me at Tahoe—

naturally when you talked about this willowy girl—well, I just never in my whole entire life read anything that was just the way I feel. You know what I mean? Did you really come from a small town? I did too. Helper, Utah. I want to be just like the way you say a girl can be, with her own apartment, all fixed up beautiful, with a wall-to-wall fulfillment bed and mirrors all over, and how there's honestly and truly nothing wrong with sleeping with all the men you like, and fixing sexy dinners for them. That recipe you gave in your 'Diet For A Super Sex Life'—you know under 'Dinners Divine'—that's where I am now, Ragout of Veal—I'm going to try that out tonight. I got this date, and I know he would . . . well, here they are—anyway, you know what I mean."

"It's *oo*," Bonner says. "Ragout."

"Oh," the salesgirl says.

The two girls come to model their bikinis before Bonner. Gloria Jean's navel is deep enough to hold a dime; the other girl's protrudes like a pearl button.

"Won't Mama just die," Gloria Jean says, turning this way and that before a triptych mirror. Her nipples press against the upper strip of cloth, and the soft swell of the pubis can be seen against the lower. She has chosen a sky blue bikini similar to the one depicted on the cover of Bonner's book.

"Who cares what she says," Doralee says, admiring her choice of zebra stripes.

"You look fabulous," Bonner says.

"That number is called Blue Lightning—that one's Over and Over," the salesgirl says.

"Perfect, perfect," Bonner says. "Look at those little fannies." She flicks her hand at Gloria Jean's hair. "Something has to be done about that bird nest. I can imagine what it would look like wet."

100   *Sans Everything*

"Oh we never go in the pool," Gloria Jean says.

Bonner strokes her chin as she walks around them. "Now you'll have to watch your posture. Let's tuck that tummy in. Pull those shoulders back. Chest out, chin up. Say to yourself I'm a swan, I'm a long stemmed rose."

"A swan, a long stemmed rose," the salesgirl says.

"Are you letting us have them?"

"Can I keep it? Please oh please."

"Sold American," Bonner nods to the salesgirl.

The girls' eyes bug. They squeal, clap, and bounce up and down on their toes. Women shoppers within earshot turn to look. "Hush now, you're young ladies."

"I'm a swan, I'm a long stemmed rose," the salesgirl says.

The girls converge on Bonner and throw their arms around her.

"You're just the kindest, most wonderfulest woman I ever met in my whole life," Doralee says.

"You said it," Gloria Jean adds, with pneumatic emphasis.

Bonner feels a pinching warmth at the top of the bridge of her nose. "Well, aren't I silly?" She pats the girls on the backsides. "Go on now, girls, I don't think they'll let you parade through the store this way."

The girls rush knock-kneed to the dressing rooms.

The salesgirl turns to Bonner. "Like I was saying, Miss Meyering—"

Bonner is backing away. "I'll have to help them with their sundresses. You know how kids are, all thumbs." Her back to the salesgirl, she rolls her eyes ceilingward.

When she returns with the girls she carries the old suits between thumb and index finger in each hand. She drops them on the counter and brushes at her hands. "Throw these out, please, dear." From her purse she draws out a fold of money held by a gold clip in the shape of a dollar-sign and hands the salesgirl a hundred dollar bill.

"They're not yours, are they?"

"No. Just little friends of mine."

"And you went and? . . . ."

For a moment Bonner thinks that the salesgirl is going to cry. She gives Bonner her change and saleslip. Bonner presses three dollars into her palm and folds her fingers over it.

"A little something for your help," Bonner says, patting her hand.

"Oh I couldn't think of taking anything from you."

"Nonsense."

Dewy sparkles shine in the salesgirl's eyes. "I'll never forget this, not in my whole entire life." She holds her cupped hands under her chin. "You wait, I'll never spend this, never. I'll put it in my book, like a flower, and whenever—"

"You do that, honey. We must dash now."

By the elevator a man bearing a sheaf of papers stops when he sees Bonner, comes to her side, and gives her arm a squeeze. "Well, what do we have here?"

Bonner glances at the girls on each side of her. They're gazing up at him. "My book ends," Bonner says.

He throws back his head and laughs, uppers and lowers. "Sharp, sharp as ever." He leans forward. "I called André's. He'll have the Tattinger chilled just the way you like it. It's still 9?"

Bonner nods.

"Fine. You haven't been to your hotel yet?"

"No, I'm just going."

He puts his hand to his mouth. His wide gold wedding band is bisected by a row of small diamonds. He whispers into her ear. "Little surprise for you." As the elevator door closes upon him he winks. "You're our big item today, Bonner."

"He's a dream," Doralee whispers. "Is he your boyfriend?"

"No, sweetie. I met him only this morning."

"Who is he?"

"His name is Mr. Pendennis. He's the manager here."

"I just adore gray temples," Gloria Jean says.

"And that dreamy tan," Doralee says.

"Get your own man," Bonner says. She laughs along with the girls and leads them to a taxicab in front of the hotel across the street. She gives the driver a bill and says, "Don't you dare let any wolves near my lambies." She hugs each girl.

They sit serenely, like Giocondas aware of some inner secret of themselves, as though from underneath their sundresses their new bikinis charge them with a sensuality that gives fullness to their lower lips, straightens their spines, swells their breasts, and puts a shine in their eyes.

From the rear window the girls wave. Bonner blows a kiss to them. She stands watching until the cab rounds the corner.

In her hotel suite she finds a vase of red roses and a printed card that reads "For our distinguished guest, Welcome to San Adelphi—Compliments of the Management, the New Mirador," and a gaudy red box from Lord's with a folded note buried in a cauliflower of red ribbon. "I can just see our big item in this little item" is written in a firm hand slantwise across the inside. She furls out a lounging gown of Italian silk in a paisley design. "Well, you went ape, didn't you," she mutters. She tosses the gown on the bed and steps out of her shoes and her dress.

At the vanity she shucks off her wig, pops out her contact lenses, peels off her eyelashes, and wipes her face clean of make-up. Along with it, a beauty mark vanishes from her right cheekbone. She studies the pores of her face and methodically applies three separate creams. She wriggles out of her panty hose and with a sigh scratches her belly and backside. Half turned to the mirror, she squeezes her bra from underneath, making light globes of her breasts, and assumes Posture #3 from her chapter on Sexual Come-ons: eyelids lowered, lower lip outthrust, chin over her shoulders. Then she unsnaps her bra, lets her breasts slide down, and scratches along the bra line underneath.

After she takes two pills, one blue and one of bright pink, and sets a tiny windup alarm by her bed for 6:20, she lies naked, admiring the girlish hollow of flesh between her hipbones. As she drifts into sleep, she seeks the reflection of herself in the bottle of pills but sees instead wavering hourglass triangles of Gloria Jean's figure, darkening, the umbilicus like a keyhole hard to find and felt for in the dark.

She comes awake, sweat on her face, at the buzzing of the alarm. She gets up, takes three Bufferin, and tries to shake away a dream that is still upon her. Leola's mother is hanging from a tree by her beads in a bottle while below Doralee and Gloria Jean are dancing to the twanging of rock guitars, as she, wearing only a blue bikini and with her hair coiffured into a tiara of plaster-white shampoo lather, runs through a gauntlet of chanting nuns to her hotel room door where Pendennis is pounding his fists and because of his demands that she pay her Lord Super Charge-Plate account on a houseful of Early American furniture which she would never have thought of buying in the first place she flies into a rage and slams the door in his face. While she comes awake, she is pushing against the door with such force that her crimson nails sink deep into the wood.

She turns her TV set up loud to drive the dream out of her head and keep it out. A robe over her shoulders, she pulls open the drapes. Shading her eyes against the brightness of the dying sun's rays, she watches the street below. From her third floor height and without her contact lenses, the traffic and pedestrians are blurred. She draws her bath. In bubbles to her chin she leisurely soaps her limbs with a bar of Elegante+. Now and then she glances through the open bathroom door at the TV, mindful of advertising that she always pays attention to. During the news her nearsightedness transubstantiates President Johnson's reddish tie into a very long tongue. She smiles at the prospect of seeing herself shortly after Easter in a testimonial commercial that she made before her departure from Hollywood for Careme Complexion soap. Her face has not been touched by a bar of soap for sixteen years. She revels in the heat of the water against her neck. In the reflection of a gilt mirror by the TV set she can make out the rich oranges and golds and antique white furnishings of her room and part of a mural that extends over her bed the width of its queen-size: one limb of a delicate tree on which sits a gold and white bird.

Through the pellmell of three television programs at her back she occupies herself with her make-up, drawn from tubes, jars, and bottles spread about her vanity. Step by step, from base coat to eyelashes, she concentrates on her face. She takes pause again and again to examine the darkening entrenchment of rings in her neck.

In her slip, carrying the wig that she has chosen to go with the green contact lenses that she now wears, she goes again to the window. Neon signs light the night so brightly as to obscure the moon and stars. Silver fishes gleam in the automobiles passing below. The late Friday night shoppers at Lord's move in fitful clumps past mannequins beckoning from jewel box windows.

Sucking on a Cert, she slips on a black sheath, puts on a pearl choker, and steps into her shoes. She stands before the mirror, palms pressed against her pelvis. Tubes tied, she never has any worries. She wants no part of the whole messy business of reproducing. At the nightstand she glances through a small datebook, making note of only the larger cities, San Francisco, Portland, Seattle, and, last on her western itinerary, Honolulu.

It's nearly 9 o'clock. She turns off the TV and an ominous quiet settles over the room. She opens the window and leans out. Night noises assail her. From the sidewalk below comes a cry and another. She recoils from what she sees in front of Lord's: a throng massed before barred windows, iron-gray doors caving in to a tree trunk borne by a thousand clawing hands, and a scarecrow being dragged under the crossarm of a telephone pole that springs up in the middle of the street. She shuts her eyes and then peers down to relocate the sources of the cries: three long-haired young men in muscle shirts and tight pants who are cutting up as they walk arm in arm under a street lamp. She closes the window. Her forehead feels cool against the glass. Like dry leaves out of the past comes a voice that she wants to forget. Why can't she expunge an old woman with no teeth and drowned eyes, hair gone, and brain so addled it is unable to tell a living woman from a dead boy? Nor can she shake away the old woman's sarcophagus of a bed where for a terrifying moment she sees herself.

A full-length mirror assures her that no such alteration threatens. Her reflection she knows better than anything in life. She is still as, no, not quite beautiful, but chic, yes, ever chic, still as charming, still as sexy. Nevertheless, questions remain to be tugged at, like a zipper stuck off track at the base of her mind. For going on six hours she has tugged sporadically and given up. She yanks the drapes hard, lights a cigarette, and paces about the room. She feels a thickening under her tongue. A dull anger begins to pound in her veins. God damn that crazy old woman. What did she really want anyway? Maybe she wasn't so crazy. Why did she?—

A soft tapping comes from the door. She gives a start. She needs to think. But she feels confused and out of control. She hates confusion. What is happening? What does that sordid, violent story out of the past have to do with her? her book? If only she could have time to think it all through. Jesus-Lord-God damned, in this day and age nobody has time for anything. Not down deep, not down at the base of the zipper where it counts. The hell with it, why should she have to think about it anyway? The tapping sounds again.

She turns to look at the bed. On the nightstand are her pills and her black eyeshade. The gown lies upon the pillows. Brimful of Tattinger, he will slaver over her. But the shade is there—it always makes night.

The voice sings falsetto three-note cheer against the door. "It's me-ee. Ba-on-ner. O-pen up. It's me-ee. Ba-on-ner."

She steps to the door, a smile fixed on her face. He stands in the doorway, tall and tan, exuding all-American get up and go get 'em and gallantly produces from behind his back a grand bouquet of madonna lilies.

THE Y

They ford the first river that runs shallow like rippling transparent muscles over a bed of light colored, egg-round pebbles. The clearing is high and dry, humped in the center and covered by stubble, sloping downward toward the juncture where a smaller river splits away to the other side from the headwater. High grazing grass flourishes in the shadows of bushy juniper that grows in an almost straight line across the top of the inverted triangle of ground. The pines above it blanket two hills in the shape of great round breasts. Low on either side, mixed with ruddy brush, quaking aspen shiver in the stillness, giving way to steep piney slopes higher up. Way off in the distance, above the span of the headwater, lie snow-topped mountains.

Duke watches his retriever sniffing along the water's edge.

"Ain't this a jewel?"

"How'd you find it?" Lew asks him.

"One day just riding around."

"Just riding around, huh?" Lew eases down and stands stretching, his palms in his back, his middle rotating. "What are the rivers?"

"I don't know, there are so many up here. I just call it the Y."

109

They unload the two horses and two mules. Duke uncinches the saddle girth on his mare, and her underside balloons out. She's warm and wet under the saddle blanket. She whinnies and nuzzles him.

"All right, mama, I know you like me."

"Downright disgusting," Lew says.

Duke grins back. "She's been like this ever since I had to help her with that foal." He leads her and one mule to water.

Lew brings the stallion that Duke has let him ride and the other mule. The stallion is acting up. Duke smacks him on the rump. "You cool down, boy."

While the animals graze below the juniper, Duke rolls out the pup tents. The canvas smells of wet leaves and boughs and smoke. He rakes his fingers through the short soft grass on the flat part of the hump. Then he sets up the tents, heads facing uphill. Each peg takes one whack. When he has the peak poles in and the canvas pulled tight, he stretches out inside his tent, cheek down, and burrows around—the ground is soft enough under the tent floor without boughs. He flips out the sleeping bags and drapes webbing over the entrances. After he has readied a pair of oil lamps, he sets out the battery lantern.

"I've seen that somewheres before," Lew says.

"Millie sent it to me last Christmas."

"Oh. Yeah." Lew resumes his wood chopping. He grunts with every blow.

Duke gets a shovel out of his gear and returns to the tents to scoop out trenches around them.

"What you doing that for?" Lew says. "Not a cloud in the sky."

"You never know."

Duke picks a spot for the fire, digs a hole, and carries rocks from the river bank. He gets the fire ready to start and puts a grate over the rocks. Three pans and the coffee pot fit on the grate. Shadows are spreading down the slopes.

"You want to eat now or wait? I can catch a couple fish."

Lew tosses down the ax. "Doesn't matter." He rotates his middle again. "My tail's so sore I can hardly move." From his pack he pulls out a bottle of bourbon. As his hand comes out, his watch band catches, snaps, and the watch falls to the ground. "Goddamnit." He picks up the watch and holds it to his ear.

"Is it okay?"

"Yeah. Just busted the band." He puts the watch in his pocket.

Duke looks at the bottle. "Little early for that, ain't it? You don't want to fish, huh?"

"Naw. I came up here to kill me a deer."

"Peel some spuds then and slice them. They're right in here."

"Putting me on KP, eh?"

"Keep you out of mischief."

Duke walks over to the other fork of the river. The tip of a fallen pine lies over the bank. Its lower branches trail in the water. The river takes a curve beyond the pine, like a leg bent at the knee. The water is slow moving, deep, and clear. He sees a trout, black dark against the clear water, shoot off in a wide angle toward the opposite side. Minnows scoot away from his feet. Then he sees another trout in one spot below him and facing upstream, its whole body shifting with the current in quick stiff tremors. He sees himself superimposed almost mirror-clear over the fish. He looks back across the clearing at the riffled river. He knows that here it's just a matter of dunking a fly. He decides to give himself ten minutes in the riffles.

Lew sits on the ground, legs spread, shoulders hunched, the bottle leaning into his crotch. He's throwing a hunting knife at a tree stump. Duke watches him: flip, thunk, lean, pull—flip, thunk, lean, pull.

"Keep that up and you're going to get it right where you live."

"That"ll be"—flip, thunk—"the day."

Duke joints his rod, threads the line, fixes the leader, and puts on a Royal Coachman. Then he pulls on his waders, turning them down above the knee, and slings his net and creel over the back of his hip. Woody follows him to the bank. He chooses a log in the river about five yards out, bone white on top, mossy green underneath, perpendicular to the bank. "Stay there, boy," he says, and wades out.

The water is shin deep and pushes against his legs. He feels the egg-round pebbles under the balls of his feet. He clinches over one with his arch and braces the other foot against the underside of the log. His casting is rusty, but he has some working room and finally lays the fly down where he wants it near the apex of the triangle. The river is almost too swift coming from the rush of the headwater, but it's clear of debris. He offers the fly again up where the bend in the Y starts. He feels the strike in his grip. He gives it a second of slack and flicks his wrist hard. The rod bows. He reels and plays it steadily. The trout slaps against the water in a curving dive into the riffles and when it comes up, spray falls away like a broken strand of pearls. It continues to stand on its tail, battling to the sides, flipping and flapping across the water until Duke nets it: a rainbow, about a three pounder, slick, firm in his wet hand below the tail. Duke examines the glassy looking eye, the gills pumping, the bright pastel and black speckle marks. "Lord, ain't you beautiful," he mutters. He whacks the trout against the log and slips it into the creel. The tail sticks out over the top. He'd like to settle for this one—he can't tolerate waste of fresh pan fish—but maybe Lew is really hungry. So he lays the fly out again in nearly the same spot and gets another strike that he doesn't feel at all first, also a rainbow, but much smaller, about eight inches. The water numbs his hands as he cleans the two fish.

When he gets back to the campsite, Lew salutes with his bottle.

"Felt good."

"I can see that all over your face." Lew lights a cigarette and takes another swig. "Want me to do anything?"

Duke looks down at the pile of half-inch thick peels and says, "Yeah, don't peel any more spuds or we'll starve up here." He lights the fire and puts on the water for coffee. He has to cut the big fish in half to cook it. He hates to do that because it ruins the bone pull when you can't lift it all the way from head to tail. Then he takes out a pound of butter and divides it into the three pans. While the butter is melting, he feeds the dog. Then he cuts up a loaf of his home-made bread into six pieces, dips them in butter, wraps the pieces in foil, and puts them near the fire. By the time the trout are cooked, the spuds and the coffee are done. He wants to keep sniffing the trout and let his mouth water at the same time. The bones pull up right anyway without taking any meat. Lew doesn't bother to wipe away the juice that runs down from his mouth.

Duke lights the lamps. He cleans his 270 while waiting for the pot of water to heat for the dishes. Lew is working listlessly at his rifle. "I don't feel so good," he says.

"You need a good night's sleep," Duke says. "Here, give me that gun."

When the dishes are finished, he walks up to look over the animals. They are settling for the night. He pats the mules and nuzzles the mare. The stallion ignores him. Lew's shadow flickers large in the firelight below. The only sound comes from rushing water. The stars get brighter in the black sky. He stretches, arms high and coming down wide, as if he's trying to take in the stars and the trees and the animals and finding at their touch that they're still not quite enough, that what he wants to touch lies somewhere back of the dark sky. "All right, keep your shirt on," he says to Woody's whine below.

At the campfire Lew sits on the tree stump, smoking, the bottle on his knee, staring into the fire.

"Sure gets dark fast in here."

"Yeah. Should be a moon later."

"Good supper."

"Thanks."

"You surprised I called you about going hunting?"

"Sure."

"How long's it been?"

"Two, three years I guess."

"When the hell they ever going to string a line to the mill? It's ridiculous. A ranger has to drive five miles to get you to the phone."

"Yeah, we're a little short on the conveniences." He looks at Lew. "I ain't been pressing you, kid. What's the matter?"

"Kid? What've you got on me, a lousy year and a half?"

"Getting pretty touchy, ain't you?" He pours himself some coffee and holds the hot tin cup in both hands.

"How's Millie? Or ain't you going to say nothing again?"

"She's all right." Lew blows smoke. "You know what I was thinking?—how you popped the question to her first."

Without a response, Duke bends to his steaming cup.

"Worst mistake she ever made, taking me instead. I sure hear enough about it all the time. But it wouldn't have worked for her. You imagine what she'd be like at a sawmill a million miles from nowhere? Got three mortgages on the house now; fancy additions and all, she still wants to keep moving up."

"How's the kid?"

"Okay. Her birthday's tomorrow. Three."

"Yeah, I know. I sent her some carvings of mine, you know, things she can play with, horses, dogs, and such. After you called, I was hoping maybe you'd bring her up as a treat or something. You ought to be there with her."

Lew slides down on the ground and faces the stump. "Naw. Got myself in a little jam. Things not going right. Stealing me blind on the lot. About two weeks ago I lost three carburetors. One Merc, they stripped everything but the engine block. Hell of a life."

"Don't the police?—"

"They're never around at the right time." He throws his knife at the stump. It sticks, then falls, and he picks it up. "Yeah, I'm in a jam all right. I got this girl to come in and work on the books about six months ago. She isn't any homecoming queen, except maybe for the eyes—got the biggest eyes, like everything's a big surprise, but she knows what she's doing with the books. Working at night, you know, part time—we're open till nine—while she's going to business school downtown. Well, one thing leads to another—never saw a girl so hungry, so . . . well, I guess she never got any affection from anybody." Lew shrugs and flips the knife. It quivers in the stump. "Yeah, it happened. She says it's mine. Hell of a life."

Duke doesn't say anything.

Lew gives him a long look. "I'm going to lay it on the line. She won't get rid of it. She can't go to her folks. They won't take her in—they go strictly by the Book. She can't stand being in that town now—come to find out she doesn't exactly like the big city. I'm strapped for cash, she hasn't got a dime. Will you let her live up at the mill till she has the kid?"

"Oh, Lew, for—"

"I told her to get rid of it, I tried and tried. All she does is cry whenever I bring it up. I mean she's religious and all that. She wants the kid . . . period."

"You going to marry her?"

"Marry her? How can I? I love Millie too much. Will you do it? I'm telling you, she's got nobody to go to."

"I'm no good around a woman, kid. I—wha'd you have to ask me a thing like this for?"

"What's a brother for if you can't ask them to help you."

"How many times do you expect me to get you out of scrapes?"

"Like when? Not this kind."

"No, I guess you never asked me to do something like this before." He stares into the empty cup in his hands. "She wouldn't like the mill. I mean, the house is all right, but . . . Ma's only woman I ever knew who could take this country."

"She's country folk. Raised on a farm." Lew watches him. "How long you expect to keep living by your lonesome?—the folks gone, Sis way off to New York. It isn't natural for you."

"It ain't? Far's I'm concerned, I'll never understand how you and Cindy can put up with city livin'."

"Okay, okay, but you know good and well you get lonesome up here."

"I get along okay. Better'n you. Things ain't near so complicated for me."

"Yeah, maybe that's what's wrong with you. You ever stop to think of that? Sure it's peaceful, but so's the North Pole."

"What's that prove?"

"People. People. That's what living is all—"

"The mill's people. Since when we ain't got people?"

"Aw, if you don't get it, I can't tell you. Look, she's a good kid. I mean it. Like I told you, she's no raving beauty, but she's nice as they come. It'd work. She'd tell her folks she went to work for my brother up in timber country, that's all. Nobody's the wiser."

"And you ain't going to marry her?"

"I can't, Duke. It'd kill Millie. You got to do it for Millie's sake, let alone me. This thing's about to tear me apart." He reaches to the fire to take out a stick to light another cigarette. As he brings it toward him, the burning end breaks off and falls on his lap. He jumps up to brush it away. Part of the stick lodges in the lower part of his hunting jacket. The fire-red tip burns the meat part of his hand. He yelps.

Duke looks at his hand. "Well, least you didn't drop the bottle." He pours cold water from a canteen into a pan and has Lew immerse the wound. Then he gets some ointment and gauze from a first aid kit in his pack and swabs and wraps Lew's hand.

"You going to be able to shoot tomorrow?"

"Nothing's going to stop me from shooting. I said I was coming up here to kill me a deer and that's what I'm going to do."

"All right, supposing I take her in. Suppose. I ain't said. What do I do when her time comes?"

"She's got a long time to go. She's not even hardly started to show yet. When . . . you won't bring her down to—well, you know what I mean."

"Now hold it, I ain't said I would yet."

"Yeah, and you haven't said you wouldn't either. You worried about the men talking?"

Duke snorts. "Let 'em talk all they want. They know who does the hiring and firing."

"Well, will you do it? You'll do it, won't you? I can count on you."

From the edge of the firelight, Duke stares into the darkness. "No, you can't count on me, not for something like this."

"What's the matter with you anyway?"

"Ain't nothing the matter with me. You got no call asking me to do it and then just going ahead and thinking I'm going and do it."

"I didn't say definitely you would, did I? At least give me some kind of an answer, yes, no, something."

"Most likely it's going to be no." He turns toward the fire. "Let me sleep on it. You better get some shuteye. We got to get up at dawn, you know." He reaches down and pulls the hunting knife out of the stump. He motions for Lew to lift his arm and shoves it into the scabbard and snaps the leather guard shut.

Lew crawls into his tent.

The fire burns low. Duke stares down into the dying embers, feeling empty, as if his backbone has been pulled out like the bone of the trout at supper. The sky darkens. Then he glimpses moonlight to the left of the breast-shaped hills, a bright moon but hidden by a veil of scudding cloud. Sure, a way to get back at her for bringing him hurt—it still cut, after all this time. Yet he knows his brother is right about what Millie's like. If she'd chosen for him, she wouldn't be at the mill now anyway—she'd have lit out long ago from the timber. No, she's where she belongs. He looks up again at the hills. The moon hasn't come out yet.

He bends down to stir the fire, and the coals seethe and snap. Let him pay for his own medicine. The stick pokes. That cut too, taking for granted, caring only for his own hide. No, let him pay, pay. The stick gouges. But that's no reason to make somebody else suffer. Aw, to hell with big eyes that are so blind they can't see. He reaches over for some of the firewood that Lew cut.

The fire starts to take on the wood. "Ain't no sign for you to go and do the wrong thing, just because you don't like somebody stomping on your toes." He can see himself as plain as day laying a clean-split log in the trough of the stove, listening to his sister bawling and his brother giggling at her, and looking up at his mother, and she, with her hand on the stove pipe damper, looking out the kitchen into the grove at the lone upright slab of pine, rounded at top, and going on, "It was him learnt it to me, and ain't a day go by I wish he was still here saying it."

The moon reappears between the two breasts of hills, brighter without cloud, spreading its light down the slopes of both hills, down the river on the left and the river on the right and the big river beyond, the water loud over the fire curling up around the logs, spreading light farther and farther out to meet the moonlight in the clearing. He stretches, rising up on the balls of his feet, arms wide and chest up, the light all around him now, feeling its warmth to the skin of his chest. The mare whinnies, maybe at the moon or maybe at the light of the fire.

"Shut up, girl," he says.

What's a stomping alongside of getting your toes mashed flat the way hers are getting mashed. And taking it—wanting the kid, no matter what, and wanting to keep it. Nobody who can fess up like that can be all wrong. He shakes his head. What right does he have to say right and wrong. Maybe there isn't any wrong and any right—maybe there's just the doing.

But Lew is dead wrong about the timber. There's nothing wrong with the timber, and what the devil does the North Pole have to do with it. No, the mill's all right. But the mill doesn't make him right just by being there. "Maybe that's what's wrong with you," Lew said. Maybe he's right. A man can be right and wrong both. Maybe the mill and people, and people and people aren't the same.

He looks in on Lew who lies stiff, his bandaged hand as white as a snowball on the outside top of his sleeping bag, and a spare sweatshirt like a patch of drifted snow in the corner of the tent.

"I'll set this lantern here for you. If you need anything else, holler."

"I'm okay," Lew says. "You decide anything?"

"No." Duke bends again. "What's her name, the girl?"

"Annabelle."

"Jesus."

Duke crawls into his tent. The sleeping bag is warm. He lies watching the play of the fire through the tent opening. The dog is stretched out on his side, his legs bracketing the fire. Duke thinks about the way he felt up near the animals while watching the stars. He thinks about the hunt the next day. His rifle feels hard against his back. He reaches around and pushes the case away from him. He thinks about having a woman around the house. He thinks about it hard. He listens to the sound the water makes and watches the light come down the other slopes. He thinks about her eyes. Hands behind his head, he watches the firelight. Annabelle. Jesus.

WHAT'S HE TO HECUBA?

When he arrives at the theater that day to perform, Laur-ence discovers that he does not know the play. Laur-ence is surprised by the large audience waiting for the play to begin. He has been rehearsing for weeks, but for reasons that he cannot explain his mind is blank. He does not have to make his entrance for some time, although he's playing the lead role. From the wings he watches the play with interest, wondering why he cannot remember his part, but he feels confident that the lines will return to him when the time comes. He has acted only a few times before, yet feels no fear. The size of the audience, somewhere between a hundred and a thousand, puzzles him.

During an intermission before his appearance, he goes for a walk. It takes him to a university library nearby where he knows he can find a copy of a play by William Shakespeare that he must have. The play he's appearing in has nothing whatever to do with Shakespeare—it's a bad play by a woman with three names, a contrived suspense-thriller, which Laur-ence takes to be a comedy. The librar-ian won't let him have the book. It's too heavy and cannot be taken out. Laur-ence becomes furious and stamps his handsome foot. The head librarian relents, and Laur-ence carries the book from the library, only to discover that the carton he has been given to hold the heavy volume is empty.

He has plenty of time to return to the theater before his appearance on stage. He is hungry but cannot find a restaurant in the immediate neighborhood. When he gets to the theater he discovers that he's very late. The director is furious with him. The play has been delayed awaiting his return. The audience is restless, as Laur-ence discovers walking down the middle aisle. He's also surprised by its number, at least 10,000. They yawn mightily and glower at him as he makes his way to the wings.

A hasty rehearsal of lines is held between Laur-ence and his leading lady, and his earlier doubts are confirmed: he has no knowledge whatever of the play in which he's appearing. However, he takes his place on stage with her. She's a sweet leading lady, with a pretty moon face and glittery eyes. She knows both her lines and his.

The curtain opens. The scene is set in the cheerful home of a young couple who are, judging by the accouter-ments of the bar, moderately well-to-do. From hints that become direct orders, Laur-ence soon finds out that the scene calls for him to make drinks for himself and the woman, who, it turns out, plays his wife. He's very glad to make the drinks and enjoys the clinking of the ice in the glasses. His wife meanwhile chatters on, and he comments occasionally, still having no comprehension of the play itself. He's not nervous—to the contrary, he's enjoying himself thoroughly.

From remarks repeated by his wife, he gathers that his part next calls for him to sit in a rocking chair alongside her where she is already rocking. During long pauses in their one-sided chat the audience coughs, but Laur-ence simply twirls his ice cubes and drinks. It's real whiskey. He mixes another for himself, skipping from the bar, for he has become slightly tipsy. His wife meanwhile is carrying on the scene, which is drawing to its conclusion. It appears from her lines that she's going somewhere, and he's supposed to kiss her goodbye. Laur-ence is still quite relaxed and easy, and no one can tell that he does not know his part. He still has no idea what the play is about, but so far it has made no difference. His replies, for all their inappropriateness, seem to belong in the conversation, although once in a while the leading lady gives him a quizzical look. Now she stands waiting with her arms out.

Laur-ence kisses her goodbye. He discovers that her lips taste wonderful, like fat bing cherries. The kiss grows longer and becomes a squirming embrace. Laur-ence can feel the hot breath of the audience riveted upon the stage. As if of its own volition, his downstage hand hoists up the back of her skirt, slides down inside the pantyhose, and grips the smooth overhang of her buttocks. She begins to grind against Laur-ence. His hand squeezes at her buttocks on both sides of the cleft. His finger begins to explore. Flushed and panting, she pulls herself away.

Laur-ence is aware that she has fallen in love with him during their embrace. She's also so skilled an actress that she can maintain her composure even as her juices bubble. She takes Laur-ence's hand and, chattering their lines, which he still does not recognize, leads him from the stage.

To the side, Laur-ence glimpses a theater critic from one of the city's newspapers. He has been warned about her in advance. She wears bangs and sits forward leering like a wolf. At that instant Laur-ence realizes that his performance will get a bad review, and so before the next act begins he is determined to learn his part.

As soon as they get off the stage, the actress lunges for him. Her fingers tear at his belt. Her passion is diverted by the director who comes at them with mottled face and bared teeth. Laur-ence however is interested in neither, for he is bent upon learning his lines. Nearby lies a book, an anthology that he knows contains the play.

Laur-ence sits down to begin to learn his lines, his mouth already working to roll out the sounds. He thumbs through the book, knowing for certain where the play is and where to look for his lines. While the woman breathes hotly on his neck and the director berates him, he searches for the play. "It's right there, Lar-ry, right there," they keep saying, and he keeps looking, but the play is not in the book.

THE WAR

It begins innocently enough with a request to subscribe to the town newspaper. The old man is out watering his lawn. The boy, walking by, stops to solicit.

"Naw," the old man says. "I take *USA Today*."

The old man's flinty stare puts the boy on edge. Shuffling, he scratches at his raggedy brown mop of hair.

"You've got to, Mister, cause if I win this contest, see, I—"

The old man curls his lip at the boy's jazzy red and yellow shirt. "Look, kid, I can't read two papers at once. I said no, that means no."

They stand almost nose to nose. The boy is short, stocky, intense; the old man once tall but now stooped, skinny, deliberate. The nozzle that separates them spreads a perpendicular fan toward the curbside.

"You ain't got nothing else to do," the boy says. "I seen you out here doing nothing, trimming them flowers, nothing."

"What you talking about, I do plenty, boy," the old man huffs. "Taking care of this big house by my lonesome—it ain't easy. You kids, you don't know what work is."

The sharpened thrust of the old man's chin eggs the boy on. "You're full of crap," he says.

The old man bristles. "Wha'd you say?"

"You heard me." The boy starts away.

The jaunty swing of the boy's shoulders urges the old man on. He knows he can let the boy's insolence go and soon the entire incident will have been forgotten. "I'm going to report you," he calls out.

The boy stops in his tracks, swings around. "Yeah, who to?"

The old man smoothes back the few wisps of white hair remaining along his widow's peak. "You got a supervisor. When he hears from me, you're not going to be doing this no more."

"You're a assho—"

"—get outta here, you little punk."

The two stand glaring at one another. The summer sun beats down, a light breeze shakes the leaves of the ash trees overhead, the cry of a child, then another child, and then another can be heard from houses to both sides.

The boy sneers and walks on as the old man turns away. Within a dozen steps the boy has already planned his revenge. One of these nights he'll stop by, pull flowers out of the boxes there on the front porch. Since he does not have anyone to give them to except his stepmother—and he wouldn't give her the time of day—he'll just scatter them along the sidewalk in front of the old man's house. He knows he shouldn't do it but he's going to anyway. In the meantime the old man, unmindful of even holding a hose, debates whether to report the boy. Common sense tells him to lay off, but he can't let the boy get away without some kind of punishment.

Later, at the same time the old man moans over the loss of his flowers, the boy curses over the loss of his job.

The old man finds out where the boy lives. It turns out that the boy's father is out of state on a demolition job, so

126   *The War*

the old man tells the boy's stepmother. She slaps the boy and locks him in, but that night he sneaks out and splatters a half-dozen eggs against the old man's car that sits in the driveway.

The old man harangues the boy's stepmother again. She calls the cops to try to scare the boy, but they can't do anything because the boy claims to be innocent. Nor can the cops help the old man the following morning. Livid in his driveway, he points to the side of his nice tidy white house with the blue trim.

"You need proof," the first cop says.

The old man's cat rubs against his legs. The old man hasn't had a chance to feed her yet—the cops have come so early.

"We can't arrest a kid on your say-so without some evidence," his partner adds.

The old man's eyes flash. His fingers become the talons of an eagle, his pecking nose the beak. "Evidence, evidence, what do you call that!" His talons stab the air.

The cops look sympathetically at a large upright middle finger painted in red. The rest of the grotesquely drawn hand bears a speckled tail down to the foundation.

"I saw him, I saw him," the old man screeches.

"You said it was dark, how could you?" the first cop says.

"He was running away." The truth be told, he awakened only in time to hear the final hissing of the spray can. By the time he got outside, the boy was gone.

Nevertheless the old man tries to have an arrest warrant made out for the boy. Nothing comes of it, except that after he comes home one evening from the store and is carrying groceries inside his house his two front tires are punctured.

In turn he spies where the boy keeps his bicycle in the back of his apartment building, sneaks over, and cuts both tires with his straight razor. Alongside the bicycle sits an overturned skateboard, one of its wheels glistening in the moonlight. He tucks the skateboard under his arm and on the way home throws it in a dumpster.

The old man does one other thing: he buys a gun.

When days pass without retaliation, the old man thinks he has won and begins to relax. He's going to put away the pistol. But then one night he hears scuffling out front. He grabs up the pistol from his bedside and runs out. Below the steps, an arm is raised, its shadow as large as a bear's. The boy is stabbing the old man's cat. The old man fires one shot.

The old man would likely be doing time if it weren't for the dead cat. Even though the boy is paralyzed from the waist down, public sentiment is placed solidly behind the old man, given the history of the boy's greater abuses against him. The local newspaper plays up the case for all it's worth.

Reporters dig into the old man's record as a railroad timekeeper before his retirement and find that he had been an ideal employee. Neighbors have only kind words for him, and admire his recovery from the loss of his wife of forty years to cancer a half-dozen years before. A daughter stationed with the Army in Germany and a son who works for an oil company in Saudi Arabia come home briefly in support of their father. The newspaper reports that he likes bingo, square dancing, bowling. He reads Louis L'Amour westerns and tries not to rely on television too much. As for the youngster, the reporters expect to find a history of juvenile delinquency. They find none. Although the boy is only a so-so student at school, he never cuts classes and is respectful toward his teachers. His dad is apologetic about the job that forces him to be gone much of the time from home. The boy says it makes no difference one way or the other. His stepmother says he watches television all the time. The boy admits that he idolizes Sylvester Stallone as Rambo. Besides the Rambo series, another of his favorite movies is *Red Dawn*. More than anything else he wants to own a motorcycle, which his father promised him once.

Setting pity for the boy aside, the judge suspends the old man's sentence on the grounds that his actions are justified. After all, a cat was killed. He delivers a stern lecture on the perils of feuding. The courtroom rings with his warning that obsessions know no bounds once they get started.

The boy has by now recuperated from his spinal wound and is getting around in his wheelchair.

On the sly over a period of time, the boy gets hold of the materials for a bomb from the demolition outfit that his dad works for. He manages to assemble it. The bomb fills his lap up to his rib cage.

Even when he has wheeled his way alongside the old man's house in the pitch dark, the boy is not quite sure exactly how to hook up the timing.

The old man, sleeping soundly, never hears a sound until the one that takes him in many directions along with his new cat and his house and his car. He is accompanied along the way by the boy and his wheelchair and some neighbors.

TO EVERY STORY

Lower Manhattan groans from the masses of tourists who
have gathered to celebrate the 100th birthday of the Statue
of Liberty. One of the busiest places at midday after the tall
ships parade is the appropriately named Tall Ships Bar and
Restaurant, located on the ground floor of the Vista International Hotel in the World Trade Center. The maitre d's
scurry about. Waiters and waitresses are sweating. It takes
a half hour for patrons to be seated, another half hour to
get a drink. They need both—they've been standing all
morning in Battery Park for the best view of the ships
passing in the harbor.

When Justin and Felicia are finally seated on the
periphery of the restaurant, Justin orders a bottle of wine.
Felicia excuses herself to join the ladies' room line that
extends halfway out into the bar. Justin looks around the
room. He has a clear view of the end of the bar that
contains tables and an elevated piano. At that precise
moment he sees a woman being seated at an opposite table
by a man bearing a red, white, and blue carryall bag. A
blue tank top and shorts emphasize the shapeliness of her
figure. Head turned up, eyes flashing white, she bestows a
dazzling smile upon the man seating her. His wedding ring
catches the light as he sets the bag on the table. She turns

her attention to another couple sitting down at their table and they begin to converse.

Justin watches her and continues to be charmed by her, yet without feeling any urgency to meet her. Her husband, oddly, bears a resemblance to Barry Coover, a friend and colleague at the Livermore Lab east of San Francisco where Justin works as a physicist. Also, she's rather young for him. She shows no particular interest in him when several times she looks across the restaurant. So he simply sits, taking in the bustle of the bar, always aware of her presence, since she sits directly opposite him.

Meredith loves the looks of the man who sits across from her. He looks 40 but is probably closer to 50. Although he's a bit too old for her—she's 37—he has a quiet grace and manliness that appeal to her. At his side a waiter is setting down a bottle of wine in an ice stand. Harold always orders mai tais or stingers or whiskey sours—drinks that she abhors. At this moment, Harold fusses beside her, trying to fix the zipper of the carryall bag. Across from her sits her friend Dolly and Dolly's husband Roc, whose actual name is Ramondo. She watches the waiter setting out two glasses at the man's table. She wonders what the person will be like who'll be joining him. She wonders what he is like. Somehow, she tells herself, she'll manage to meet this man.

Justin glances at a theater directory that he has clipped out of the *Times*. A rare bird for a scientist, he likes ballet, plays, classical music, art galleries, museums, and musicals. He is trying to decide among *The Mystery of Edwin Drood, Big River,* and *Sweet Charity* if tickets are available for a Sunday matinee.

His companion Felicia, joining him now at the table, depends upon him for all such recommendations. As a tough-minded, driven business woman, she remains largely indifferent to the fine arts. She owns and operates a string of pre-kindergarten schools, branching out from the home base in Livermore to others in Danville, Pleasanton, Fremont, and Milpitas. Justin persuaded her to put down her plans for yet another school in San Jose to come on vacation. Now she's glad she did. They are entering their third week on holiday, having spent ten days in Washington, D. C., and at a duned beach in North Carolina. Like Justin, she's divorced. Both of them have grown children. His three are older than her twins who are college students. She's a fine handsome woman, although Justin wishes she'd have more meat on her bones. She loves him very much, but Justin himself is experiencing a problem that he keeps hidden. After four years with her, he's getting bored.

So that's what she looks like, Meredith gloats, watching the woman come to his table and take her seat. Pretty, with those gaunt cheekbones and that champagne-colored hair, but, my god, downright anorexic-looking. What must a man feel like making love to a skeleton? And she better get out of the sun, or her skin is going to turn to leather. California probably, or maybe Florida. From her vantage point, Meredith can see his face and the woman's back directly over Harold's shoulder. She's unable to make out any wedding rings. She'll have to get closer to make sure, although she really doesn't care if he's married or not.

She's ready to scream at Harold. She said nothing in the morning when he put on his red, white, and blue sports shirt; white shorts; red, white, and blue socks; and a blue-billed cap divided into—guess what?—a tricolor crown. Sure, it's a patriotic occasion and if he feels like becoming a walking flag, fine. But then he had to stuff the carryall bag to capacity—in spite of its defective zipper—so that it won't close. Now at the table he can't stop fussing with it. Over and over he struggles with the zipper. He has that quality of stick-to-itiveness that drives her wacky. When he makes up his mind to complete a task, nothing can deter him: earthquake, typhoon, intercontinental warfare. So while everybody chats about the heat, the crowd, the tall ships, he concentrates on the zipper. Drinks are ordered— he works on the zipper. Drinks come—he takes a sip of his mai tai and fights the zipper. Drinks are consumed, another round delivered, and, victory, he conquers the zipper.

Roc whistles, Dolly cheers, and Meredith reaches over to clap him on the shoulder. Harold beams when Roc says, "Gotta hand it to you, Hal, you got the touch."

"And the patience . . . the patience," Meredith says.

"Except what happens when you have to open it," Dolly says. "Are you going to start all over?"

Felicia is bubbling with good cheer. Justin enjoys her company in such times.

Ordinarily they would be impatient with the service, but they're tired from their long standing wait for the tall ships. Both of them are glad to be able to sit where it's cool and comfortable. They don't care if the lunch lasts for three hours, and it seems headed that way. A contributing reason is Justin's meal. He has ordered the chef's special diced salad, and now he's making a joke of eating with elaborate preciseness each piece of ham. They laugh when one of the maitre d's comes to replace the lunch menu with the dinner menu.

"The sun will go down, night will fall, and you'll still be nibbling like a squirrel at that salad."

He continues to laugh. "And morning will come and we'll still be here and they'll deliver the breakfast menu and . . . ."

While Felicia is laughing, Justin looks over her shoulder at the woman who is talking away merrily to the friend across her table. She is moving her arms, gesturing with her hands and fingers. Her eyes sparkle. He can't stop watching her.

For the first time in months, Meredith isn't bored. Coming up to New York for the Liberty weekend to stay with Dolly and Roc has lifted her spirits. One can play only so much tennis and golf, swim only so many laps, read so many current novels before restlessness sets in. She loves musical comedies and ballet, and doesn't get enough of either. She wants to frequent the National Gallery and the Hirshhorn Gallery more often, but inertia has kept her at home in Alexandria.

It's nice of Harold not to want her to work, but she has too much time on her hands. She doesn't mind so much that he's never home. Their interests hardly match, starting with his computers and his printouts from his job as middle manager at GSO. And he has another passion: sailing. In his every spare moment, he's on the Potomac. His enthusiasm dims hers. They have no children, nor does she intend any by him. She has had one brief affair with her dentist, who made her perfect caps. She wonders often why she married Harold, while fully aware that she took him on the rebound from a failed first marriage, which included a painful miscarriage. In most ways he's a very nice man—he drives her wacky, that's all. As much as she wants children, she knows she will continue on the Pill. Now she amuses herself by imagining that at her first opportunity, here in the Tall Ships Restaurant, she will go up to this man whose looks she likes so much and she will shout in the smoky, manic voice of Catherine O'Hara doing Lola Heatherton: "I'll bear your child, let me bear your child."

When lunch dishes are being taken away, Felicia excuses herself again. Justin has stopped kidding her about her ten-cent kidneys; the joke has worn thin. He looks at the woman opposite him. He wishes that he could meet her, but he has no skills at flirting. He sits.

Although Meredith knows that she's attractive, she won't foist herself on him. Such behavior would cheapen her. What is she to do? She wants to meet him, without seeming brazen. She's no pickup—the thought of making herself available repels her. She wishes, though, that Harold and Dolly and Roc were not at her table. She glances at the man opposite her. He sits, expressionless. A pianist has come to entertain the crowd. His rendition of the theme from *Arthur* can barely be heard above the din.

She would be wild in bed, he thinks. Fleshy, curvaceous. Felicia is all bones and sharp angles. Her innominate bones bring to his mind images of concentration camp survivors. Sometimes her pelvis actually hurts him.

He would have great control making love, she says to herself. He would take hours and leave her exhausted and limp. Harold's maximum is ten minutes, the usual, five. He snores while she tosses. She is tired of being left unfulfilled.

She takes a deep breath and starts to get up to try to meet him, but she thinks she sees the skeleton coming so she sits back down. In the meantime he heads through the bar. She enjoys watching him move. He's taller than she had thought.

When Justin comes back from the men's room he looks toward her, expecting to exchange looks with her, but she is turned and talking to her male friend. Her husband is gone. His bag sits on the table. The pianist is playing "My Funny Valentine." No one seems to be paying any attention to the music.

Justin returns to his table to finish the rest of his wine. The woman moves toward him, yet without looking at him. She's straight-backed, graceful, bustier than she looked at a distance. She stands near her male friend, chatting, not more than six feet away. Close up, she's even more attractive: moist full lips, high color at cheekbones, liquid eyes. He likes her dark, thick hair, her clean features. Her glance sweeps past him around the restaurant. He has misunderstood. She is not interested in him at all. He says nothing and drinks his wine. He watches her lean her arm out against a partition separating the bar from the restaurant. He can see the top edge of her brassiere and the rounding flesh above it.

Why doesn't he say something to me? Meredith asks herself. Why doesn't Roc go away for a minute? She raises her arm again in frustration, her glance sweeping below to him, then to other diners. He's not interested. Why? She wants to touch his wavy silvery hair. She loves his eyes. They are large and dark and black browed. But they look right through her. His face is absolutely blank. What do I have to do? she asks herself. Fire off a flare?

Harold joins her. "I made the call," he says. "We can go there anytime."

She follows him outside. Enough, she groans to herself when she reaches the sidewalk. She knows now her opportunity will be lost unless she speaks to this man she has fixed upon. She tells Harold that she has forgotten her hair brush and charges back into the entryway of the hotel. He is still alone. The skeleton has not returned. She slows within a few yards of his side. She will ask his name, his address, that's all. No, she will tell him she thinks she met him once at a party . . . she will . . . she quails. She stops, six feet behind him, then turns her back so as not to embarrass herself.

Out of the corner of his eye, Justin sees the woman. At first she looks intent upon approaching him, but then she stops and turns away, eyes downcast, as if she has remembered something, so he is most likely not the object of her attention. Nevertheless, he rises to say something to her, as the pianist plays the opening bars of "Tomorrow." At that moment, Felicia returns, giving him a big smile.

On the sidewalk Meredith stands with Harold and Dolly and Roc who are debating what they should do: take in some more of the Harbor Festival or head out now for their friend's boat in New Jersey for viewing the later fireworks. In her dejected state, she doesn't care what they choose to do. She is still thinking about her abortive attempt to meet the stranger. What a mess she has made of it. She's almost ill from the strain of her missed opportunity.

When Justin comes out of the bar with Felicia on his arm, he sees the woman standing with her husband and her friends at the edge of the sidewalk. She is in the middle of a triangle they have formed. He senses that she is staring directly at him, but he cannot look again at her because he

To Every Story

is ashamed of making more of their near encounter than really existed. Since she isn't interested in him, he needs to prove that he doesn't have to meet her. So he intentionally ignores her. He takes Felicia's arm and guides her up the block.

She stands chewing her lip, terribly disappointed that he has not even smiled or made any attempt to acknowledge her. She feels terrible as she watches him walking up the street with that cadaver. How could he not be interested in me? she asks herself. She wants to shout at him that he's stupid. She hates him. He doesn't deserve me, she tells herself. The hell with him.

At the end of the block he realizes that he has made an awful mistake. Felicia is saying that in spite of the heat she is glad to be out of doors and walking around again. He pays her no heed—his mind is totally absorbed. The shock of his stupidity, his timidity, his silence, his apathy over-whelms him. Why hadn't he done anything? Why hadn't he at least spoken to her? Why had he been so slow? How ridiculous that a man his age should behave like a shy teenager. Anybody with any brains could have sensed that she wanted to meet him. He knows with utter certainty that she had come back into the restaurant for that purpose. He savors her look of determination as she came toward him.

But was she coming to meet him? No, not really, he tells himself. He is making up her attraction to him. She had come closer to him and, sizing him up, decided that she wasn't interested. She saw how old and unappealing he really was. That explained why she hadn't smiled or spoken. But she had been near him earlier. So why had she come back toward him? To meet him, of course. But she had to turn away because how could a woman be expected to maintain her decorum in . . . no, it was his job to establish contact, and he ruined the chance.

He guides Felicia back in the direction from which they have come. She doesn't mind—they are merely strolling anyway. The woman and her party are gone. The crushing reality of the lost moment strikes him. She is lost forever. He feels devastated. Yet there's still a possibility that he might run into her again. While he is buoyed, he remains depressed.

Meredith suffers a barrage of conflicting feelings. While frustrated by the loss, she's gladdened, if not relieved, because her life remains secure and uncomplicated. At the same time she's embarrassed by her schoolgirlishness and angry with her own temerity. As they stop here and there in Battery Park, she notices how easily people talk to one another in festive times. A slip of a girl in a T-shirt bearing a replica of the Statue of Liberty above NEW YORK CITY begins an easy conversation with a young man beside her. Soon they are exchanging confidences. Perhaps they will drift apart, perhaps not, but a contact has been made. Why can't she slip out of the conventional mold in which she has been raised: the assumption that the man always makes the initial advance? It's a stupid tradition. Yet she can't help it. You simply can't throw yourself at a stranger. What nonsense. "Throw yourself" sounds as if it has come from some ludicrous melodrama. Yet she cannot forgive herself for quailing near his side. And she feels miserable.

Wandering through the Harbor Festival, Justin is lost in thought. He ignores music coming from a Latin American salsa band high up on a stage in a plaza. As he strolls with Felicia along Whitehall and they turn back along State Street, he pays little attention to the swirling crowd and congested vendors' booths. Felicia is used to his occasional removal and doesn't seem concerned about his silence.

He tries to remember the details of a story he had read many years before for a college class. Some army officer—he can't remember in what country—had been kissed in the dark by a woman who mistook him for her lover. All Justin can remember is that the officer had a mustache like a lynx and that he had acted like a boob for weeks afterward by creating a fantasy life out of nothing. Now here he's doing the same thing.

What could be accomplished in a brief meeting anyway? Meredith asks herself as she sits in the back seat of Roc's car on the way to New Jersey. Not much, she knows. Still, she's tantalized by who he is, what he does for a living, what his life is like. They could have written, telephoned, but how much? There would be the wife or girlfriend to put up with, secretaries to work through, children to avoid—it would all get so messy. Maybe it's for the better that they failed to meet. But a powerful sense of loss sets in again, and she feels worse.

And then Justin remembers another one. He had been a very young lieutenant sent to New Jersey for special training before going off to fight in the last year of the Korean War. On a day off he had been in downtown Manhattan. He was headed into the subway and she was coming up the stairs, a vision, in yellow, in a wide-brimmed hat, tall, statuesque, a model perhaps or an actress. She looked at him straight on, neither unfriendly nor flirtatious, merely an open direct look, a bit quizzical maybe, a face open to possibilities. He was stunned by her beauty. Hat bill pushed low, almost to his nose, he stared at her. She reached the top of the stairs. He hadn't yet started down. He turned, wanting to say something as she passed. She seemed to hesitate a moment too. His mouth parted. His reserve prevented speech. She didn't shrug or frown or do anything except move on. He turned to follow but couldn't bring himself to go after her. Such an act was gauche, undignified, creepy. So he let the moment pass, regretting it for a time. One day he happened upon a quotation by Izaak Walton: "No man can lose what he never had." If the advice helped him then, it doesn't console him now. He feels cheated again by the loss, robbed, stripped of a fuller life.

That night in Sam Perl's boat Meredith lies back watching the fireworks in the company of a dozen acquaintances. She has never seen fireworks so spectacular and so prolonged. She wishes she were watching it with him. Then it's off to bed at Dolly's and Roc's place. She falls asleep thinking of the man's silvery hair and his piercing eyes.

Justin and Felicia take a short subway ride up to Chambers Street for the fireworks display. He forces himself not to let his mind wander. He concentrates on watching the fireworks. He is solicitous of Felicia and sees to it that they get right back on the subway before the crush begins. Their destination is an apartment on West 82nd. Justin's old friend Grady Haloran, who is curator at the Museum of Natural History, has gone on a combination business and pleasure trip to Europe and turned over the key. A strange sight greets them in the crowded, graffiti-laden subway car. Sitting below them is a young woman dressed as a clown: red wig, bulbous nose, baggy pants. A huge smile is painted on her face, but she's crying. She makes no sound, even when the car is at a silent stop. Large tears course down her cheeks and disappear under her jaw bone. She blinks repeatedly. She has not moved when they get off at their stop.

As Justin holds Felicia in bed and she falls asleep on his arm, he thinks about the woman in the bar and about the clown.

When Meredith awakens in the morning she lies in bed thinking about men in her life that she remembers vividly but never met personally. One time before her miscarriage when out driving she had passed a street repair crew. A blond, curly-haired, thick-chested worker, tanned golden, was manning a jackhammer. As she slowly drove by, he let up on the jackhammer, reached up to wipe his brow, saw her, and winked. She had never forgotten that wink. Now that she prefers older men, she chides the one in the restaurant who wouldn't let up his inhibitions enough to do the same. Then there had been that customer at the boat show who was a ringer for Ted Danson in rimless glasses, and also that airline pilot at Dulles, and that surfer in Hawaii.

There will be others to meet, she knows, as she goes downstairs to have orange juice. And yet she'll always look back with regret at this missed opportunity. We all search for the ideal mate, she tells herself. No matter how many mates we try, first or fourth or eleventh, we keep on searching, knowing the search will never end, settling for less than what we want, staying married to people that we come to love less and less, always hunting for, praying for—no, that's too strong a term, she thinks—yearning for the ultimate intimacy, the absolute commitment, the perfect match.

Harold comes down the stairs, in search of his coffee, yawning and scratching his crotch. Meredith feels tears start to form, but she won't let herself cry.

Justin feels miserable upon awakening. It's only six o'clock. He slips out of bed and goes to the window to look out over an empty street. She has disappeared into the face of the republic, irretrievably lost. He cannot adjust to his disappointment of the missed opportunity, and is overcome by a general sense of depression. He wants her to be miserable, like himself. He sighs and begins to pace.

You never get what you want for yourself in life, he placates himself. Except for a lucky few. A fraction of one percent, if that. The rest of us—he sets an arbitrary figure of 99.9+%—always get less than what we want in educations, jobs, professions, mates, children, homes, friends, and, most of all, in accomplishments. No person, unless a fool, believes he has accomplished what he wanted to in a lifetime. Justin remembers reading of famous men and women who all confessed—each after a lifetime of great achievement—that they had fallen short of their aspirations. It's always so, he mutters, as he turns back to the bedroom, and you must reconcile yourself to the hard truth of it. What you make of your life in the face of these disappointments matters most of all. After all, isn't it the *process* that counts, rather than the goals?

Meredith spends Saturday morning in long lines of people crawling around tall ships. That damned Harold and his passion for sailing. He spends so long on the tall ships that they have a late snack luncheon beside the indoor waterfall of the Trump Tower, and to make up to her he lets her shop at Bergdorf Goodman where she spends so much money that the rest of the evening is spoiled. But the evening is a bust anyway because by the time they get to Central Park for the classical concert, they are so far back they can hardly see the stage over the sea of people numbering, they are later to learn, 800,000, and both of them go to bed in a foul mood and not speaking.

Justin and Felicia have a full day: lunch in Rockefeller Center, then up to Lincoln Center to see a matinee of the ballet *Giselle*, then off to Central Park for the lawn concert where they manage to make their way toward the front near the stage. Justin ingratiates himself to a tawny-haired young woman seated on a satin blanket. A well-trained Russian wolfhound sits beside her. She is willing to share her blanket with them, in lieu of a friend she awaits who is late. As darkness falls during the concert she lights perfumed candles and pours chilled wine. To mask her jealousy and disdain, Felicia pretends to be totally absorbed in the performances of Placido Domingo and Itzhak Perlman and a half dozen other performers and the introductions of them by Angela Lansbury and Kirk Douglas. The crowd is infuriated by the noise of a helicopter flying a Burger King ad directly overhead. At the end of the concert when fireworks erupt, Scheherazade, the wolfhound, panics, and Justin has to use all his strength to hold her down. Maia, her owner, is grateful to Justin and thanks him profusely as they part company. Walking toward their apartment in the dense crowd, Felicia is cold to Justin. In the elevator by themselves, he asks her what's wrong. She hisses that he's a fool for turning on the charm with a fancy whore, to which Justin replies, "It got us a place to sit up close, didn't it?" Later as they snuggle, she softens toward him, and he makes love to her gravely and tenderly. As he falls asleep, his mind is again on the young woman coming toward him at his seat in the restaurant.

On Sunday, Meredith and Harold plan to take in a matinee of *Sweet Charity* in Manhattan and then drive back to New Jersey for the Liberty Weekend Closing Ceremonies in the Meadowlands. They pack ahead of time because they'll leave for home from the stadium. Dolly and Roc don't say anything but are miffed at not being invited along for the day. The problem is that they expect Harold to buy the tickets, and he isn't about to spend another two hundred dollars. So in spite of hugs all around, the parting of friends isn't entirely amicable.

Meredith and Harold have a good time at the musical, grab a bite nearby, and are in their stadium seats at 7:30, leaving plenty of time for Harold to set up his movie camera. The break allows Meredith time to make her way to a ladies' room. Of course she doesn't see the silvery-haired man anywhere. During an audience participation trick with flashlights, she asks herself if he too is flashing his light. She has almost given up all hopes of ever seeing him again, yet she hasn't been able to get him out of her mind.

Meredith loves the musical panorama of jazz and rock 'n' roll and country and gospel and Hollywood themes and Broadway show tunes. She is delighted by the high-spirited caterwauling of Patti LaBelle, the classiness of Shirley MacLaine, the exuberance of the purple, red, and green spangled Pointer Sisters, the climactic belting of "New York, New York" by Liza Minnelli. At the finale of the ceremonies when the stadium floor is filled with a thousand participants who form a map of the USA, she wistfully ponders, as the choir sings the words "America, America," where home is for the man she so desperately wanted to meet.

Justin and Felicia enjoy *The Mystery of Edwin Drood* and laugh often at its inspired silliness. Then they take a bus from the Port Authority for the closing ceremonies at

Giants stadium. Justin has given up searching for the woman he is smitten by. He is, after all, a realist. But a romantic part of him still believes that he might by chance find her. He excuses himself to seek out a concessions counter. The woman is nowhere to be seen.

The ceremonies put him in a bemused frame of mind. He chuckles at the excesses of showmanship that surpass ordinary glitz to become superglitz. As in the recent Olympics, patriotism has verged into jingoism. Sheer numbers overwhelm the audience: a waving American flag formed by hundreds of red, white, and blue caped dancers, a five-hundred member "Statue of Liberty All-American Marching Band" made up of college musicians from around the country, scores of Elvis Presley impersonators, dozens of square dancers and banjo players and fiddlers, at least two hundred tap dancers, half of them on the multi-tiered stage, the rest of them down on the field, each tapping away on her own platformed star; a cast of thousands performing to gushing water fountains and stirring patriotic songs and leaping laser beams. When the huge choir intones "Remember, Rejoice, Renew," Justin takes the refrain personally and finds no solace in it. And while he is aware of the joy of the celebration, joy, joy, and more joy, everywhere, he asks himself how a man and a woman meant to be matched can be left so miserable in their frustration at not meeting. In posing such a question, he knows he is an utter fool.

Meredith talks Harold into stopping along the way in New Jersey. They are too tired to drive half the night. Since Harold has an extra day off on Monday, there's no need for them to be at home. Harold is strangely withdrawn, but she doesn't pay much attention. They find a motel and crash.

Justin's last chance is coming up. He will find the woman at the Kennedy terminal when he and Felicia arrive for their flight to San Francisco. It's a long shot, but it can happen, to be sure, in the same way as winning at the lottery in New York or California.

She is not at the terminal.

When the plane is in the air, he sighs and puts his hand on Felicia's thigh. She smiles, pleased by his show of affection. He feels guilt about the way he has removed himself from her. Although he has been acting foolish and knows it, he can't seem to help himself. His mood worsens, this time for a reason that is clear to him. The other woman's face is slipping away from him. What exactly did she look like? He tries to associate her with some celebrity and can't. He remembers only the top of her right breast above her tank top when she leaned against the partition near him. Yet her husband's face remains indelible because he looks so much like Barry Coover. The irony strikes him hard: he will forget entirely the woman's face, but he will always be half-heartedly on the watch for the husband because of his resemblance to a friend. He feels a bitterness rising from the pit of his stomach.

On the way home to Alexandria, Meredith bestows a smile on her husband as he drives, but then turns her head aside to frown. She can no longer remember precisely what the man in the restaurant looks like. She guesses that six months later she might recall only his shock of silvery gray hair and maybe the way his light blue trousers fit snugly around his lean hips.

She will meet the right one someday. He has to be out there. He has to be. She is sensible enough to know that a woman can be compatible with any number of different men. And vice versa. Teeth clenched, she talks to herself. The major difficulty you face as a woman is finding the man who is right for you, without having to endure the degrading process of advertising yourself. They're all over the place. They are, they are. But, where? My god, where?

Head tilted back, Justin feigns sleep. He will keep searching for her, the ideal woman. He will find her, one of these days. Then he reckons, mouth twisted in a smile of rueful irony, when it will probably occur: on his final bed. She'll be all in white, arms out, ready to take care of him, beckoning, taking him in, and just at that moment when ready to touch, to embrace, to kiss, she will begin to fade in his vision . . . fade and fade, all white.

The car zips south along the turnpike. Meredith sleeps, and when she awakens she sees off in the distance through the fuzzy veil of her eyelashes the shining Washington monument.

Justin's plane soars west, high above the clouds, into a vast blue bowl of sky.

HOW CHARLIE THE LIZARD
BECAME A GOOD BOY

On the Strip, Charlie the Lizard is doing the wife of Rhino Neck, which Rhino Neck does not know.

Louise B's B, the looker that is Rhino Neck's wife, has this name because she is everywhere soft as a baby's butt. When she is in flagrante with Charlie the Lizard she discovers that he is indeed tattooed as a lizard in all of his many places: wrists, arms, legs, chest, and beyond.

One day she is in the throes of making it with Rhino Neck and she yells Oh You Lizard You Are Some Lizard OOOOOOO I Like That You Big Lizard Head. Naturally this makes an impression upon Rhino Neck, which he remembers as he has been told he is many things but never a lizard.

One night after making it with Louise B's B, Charlie the Lizard does a large amount of skimming at the casino, which is under the thumb of C-O-D Greek, as he is called, C-O-D standing not for Cash-On-Delivery as anybody might conclude but instead for Concrete-Over-Dose, which he has been known to administer to parties he is not crazy about. Charlie the Lizard disguises the skimmings with some of his own winnings from the tables after work. He is carrying with him many thousands of dollars in money in a zippered bank-deposit purse.

151

C-O-D Greek, who is in the company of Rhino Neck, says, Charlie the Lizard where have you been we have not seen you in a time.

Charlie the Lizard says, I have been to the bank where I obtained a glorious treasure.

C-O-D Greek says, Is this a treasure you wish to show me?

Charlie the Lizard unzips the purse and then thinks the better of it. The reason is, the room key of Louise B's B is in the midst of the money stash. Rhino Neck would surely recognize the key as it is of a large flat metal card type of a special powder bluish nature in its own special clear plastic jewels case with pink felt bed and the number 3396 besides. Charlie the Lizard sighs and says, No, I must not.

So C-O-D Greek begins to goad Rhino Neck: You are supposed to be a Big Man on the Campus of Life. Why do you not have him show you his treasure?

I will do this, says Rhino Neck, extracting his blade.

But before he can do so, Charlie the Lizard is sawing with his own blade at Rhino Neck's gizzard. Because of his horny plating, Rhino Neck does not go easy. As he is gurgling away his last minute on the Campus of Life and Charlie the Lizard is still sawing away at his gizzard, Rhino Neck sees the upper arm and wrist of Charlie the Lizard below his busted tux sleeve. Wide eyes fading of light, he gurgles, The Lizard, The Lizard, and down he falls like a fat palm tree.

See what you have put me up to, says Charlie the Lizard, offended. Was this necessary? He was not too smart, but he was not a bad sort.

Charlie the Lizard indignantly adjusts his tux.

You are right, says C-O-D Greek. Except he was no longer of any use, as he has been doing skimming on me. You saved me the trouble of gnocching him.

C-O-D Greek hands Charlie the Lizard his money purse.

I picked up your money so as not to have it wetted by the blood, he says. Of course he has seen the key and recognizes it, having himself on occasion made use of it. But C-O-D Greek, known for his good sense, has the good sense to keep his mouth shut.

Charlie the Lizard does not know C-O-D Greek knows about the key, which now makes no differences anyways as Louise B's B door will always be open. What Charlie the Lizard does know is that C-O-D Greek has seen the skimmings and he has the good sense to cease and desist at that moment. His look lets C-O-D Greek know that he will be a good boy forever more.

OVERCOME

In his pork-pie hat, sport coat, and tie, the tiny black boy looks like a miniature adult, yet he's only about five years old. Save for a change of shirt he has worn the same outfit every day for more than two weeks. He sits in the chair against the wall, swinging one leg, eyes white to the left on his mother. She ignores the child and sits staring at a point above the left corner of Laxalt's desk.

"Do you bring him to all your classes?" Laxalt asks.

"Can't afford no babysitter," she says.

"Well, I've never had a mother bring her child to a class of mine."

The woman glances at her son and around Laxalt's office before settling once again at that focal point near his desk. "He mind," she says. "He don't bother nobody. If'n he do I beat his butt."

"He's fine," Laxalt says. "Now, let's get down to business. You're going to be a teacher, you said. At what level?"

"High school. I'm a aide right now."

"Oh, where?"

"Lincoln. Miz Oates my supervise."

"And what will you be teaching?"

"English."

155

Laxalt puts his elbows on the desk. His fingers form a church steeple below his nose. "English?"

She stares back at him as if he were muddle-headed. He glances down at the paper on his desk—her first. His worst fears are being confirmed.

"What year are you?"

"Senior. 'bout to graduate. Only need this here course."

"You've had English before."

"At the JC. Got *A*s twicet."

"You dropped your first course there. Why?"

Her nose crinkles. "How come you find that out?"

"I looked at your transcript. Who taught that first Comp?"

"I doan 'member. Some woman. She didn't learn us nothin. S'why I gived up. Couldn't understand nothin she say."

"I see, so you took your Comp from?—"

"Mr. Hobart. Bes teacher in the whole school."

"And you did a lot of writing for him?"

"Huh?" She looks sideways. "Orenthal, you be still. The man's talkin."

He smiles at the boy twitching in the chair beside her. "Papers. Your essays, themes. How did he grade them?"

She looks at him blankly and shrugs. "Didn't have to write nothin."

"What did you do?"

"Seen movies."

"You went to movies in a composition course?"

"He say we got to learn about movies, TV, talk about 'em."

"And he gave you *A* grades."

"Never missed no class. I seen ever one of them pitchers."

"Let me get this straight. You took a whole year of English and never wrote anything. Did you study grammar, mechanics?"

"Doan get you. What English got to do wif mechanics?"

He leans back, silent for a moment, studying her. The sullenness of her pout unnerves him. "I don't suppose you did any writing in high school?" The question hovers unanswered. His fingers join to form another church steeple. "So you want to be an English teacher. You're going into a high school to try to teach your students to express themselves correctly, lucidly."

"Thas right, I'm gonna be a teacher. Ain't nothin going to stop me neither."

"But you don't write well, to put it mildly. This paper is atrocious. Can you teach English when you don't know the fundamentals, when you can't even write a decent sentence."

She clenches her jaw. "I don't write no dirty sentence."

"You misunderstand."

She draws herself upright in her chair and speaks as she rises. "Well, I'm goin to be a teacher and nobody, I mean nobody, ain't goin to stop me. Come on, Orenthal, we got to git to Lincoln." She yanks the boy after her and he shoots out the door like the tail of a kite.

That evening at dinner Frank tells his wife about the black woman's determination to teach. "And can you imagine, she's a functional illiterate."

"Monte, Evi, come on you turkeys, settle down." Annie finishes ladling soup and furrows her brow at the children until they stop their horseplay. "Do you think she'll teach?"

"Over my corpse she will."

"If she graduates and gets her credential, you can't stop her."

"She has to pass my course to meet the ed. requirement. She won't make it."

"You know already?"

"All you have to do is look at her paper."

"Maybe she'll get better."

"Not a chance, Annie. This girl missed the train, starting way back in grade school."

"So let's say she doesn't get by you—she'll just try somebody else in the department."

"I'll spread the word about her." Frank crumbles two crackers in his soup. "There's another problem. I think she's a touch loony."

"Oh dear," his wife says.

"Not bonkers outright, but on the edge. One thing, she's sure paranoid about me."

Monte wants to know what *paranoid* means.

Frank explains the word, then looks from his son to his daughter. "They're the ones who are going to suffer. What happens when they get to high school and know more than their teachers?"

"What are you going to do?"

"I'll start at the School of Education tomorrow. Somebody's got to do what has to be done."

Dean Thurstone slides a piece of paper across his desk to Laxalt. "Bill Doobey sent it to me the other day—he's a principal over at Kennedy. We got an epidemic on our hands."

Laxalt reads:

KENNEDY JUNIOR HIGH SCHOOL

Substitute Rating Form

Check Yes or No for each item below and comment where necessary. Return form to main office upon completion.

✓ Rollbook
_____   _____
Yes   No

✓ Seating Chart
_____   _____
Yes   No

✓ Prepared Lessons
_____   _____
Yes   No

Cooperative students _____All_____-

Uncooperative students _____L. Alverez_____-

Your comments

Good day. No probelams.
✱ Wrote this to soon.

Any additional explanation

✱ I blue-slipped. L. Alverez Per. 2
he borrow a pensil because I did'nt
have change and at the end of the
period I asked if he had finish the
assignm. and did he want his gt. back
he threw the pensil on my desk, I gave
him his quarter and leaving my desk
he call me a nigger! I then saw
red and sent him to the Principle.

Signature,   Date
Raynette Harrell   2/2

Overcome   159

"Oh God," Laxalt says.

Dean Thurstone nods. "Sad, huh? No, worse than sad. That sub took a credential here a couple of years ago. Any day now she'll find a full-time job. She's attractive, she's young, she's nice . . . and she's an absolute dumbbell." The Dean gazes out the window. "I've never seen such colors at this time of the year." He turns back to Laxalt and adds with the trace of a smile. "You know what she teaches of course."

"Don't tell me. English."

"Bingo."

"How did she get that far?"

"It happens," the Dean sighs. "At least now we've got the state proficiency tests."

"But that's too late," Laxalt protests. "Why let them go on, then zap them when they're getting ready to teach?"

Again the Dean gazes out the window, upper teeth on his knuckles. "And what about the ones already teaching?—so far, we can't touch them."

"Well, Victorene Jenkins isn't going to be one of them."

"We'll have to put a check on her."

"Is that all? Can't I see somebody about her? She must have a supervisor or adviser over here."

Reddening, Dean Thurstone flips through a file. "T. Heebert Easter. I'll have my secretary arrange a conference for you."

At the door Laxalt turns. "What's the *T.* stand for?"

The Dean cocks an ear as if he hasn't understood.

"I'm always curious about first initials," Laxalt says. "You know, J. Alfred Prufrock. You said, *T.* Heebert Easter. I just wanted to know what the . . . ." He lets his voice trail away.

The Dean turns to another set of files. "Terdell. Why are you smiling?"

"No reason," Laxalt says.

T. Heebert Easter knows who he is and wants everybody else to know. A black and white puptent sign on his desk bears his name above ASSOCIATE PROFESSOR, CURRICULUM AND INSTRUCTION. His degrees hang under glass in metallic gold frames on a side wall: B. A. Howard University, M. A. Arizona State University, Ed. D. Wayne State University. Laxalt has never seen him on the campus. Easter wears a three-piece glen plaid suit and a ruby stick pin in his tie. The triangular shape of his mocha-colored face is accentuated by his gaunt cheeks and long fuzzy sideburns. Hair has receded along the two sides of the crown so that what's left on top resembles the tuft of a peacock. He keeps standing, so Laxalt stands.

At Laxalt's complaint about his charge, Easter asks for proof, and Laxalt thrusts Victorene's first paper at him.

Easter gives it a quick look. "I've seen worse. It's not so bad." He runs a hand over his peacock tuft of hair.

"Not so bad? It's awful."

"There's other things 'sides writing." Easter returns the paper. "You seen her in the classroom? The kids get along with her jus fine. She's mature, experienced. We need teachers like her."

"We don't need any illiterates, and we don't need a potential psycho either."

"You in the psychologizing business, too, huh." Easter looks him up and down. "Don't s'pose her being black got anything to do with your getting up on your high horse."

Laxalt feels his blood race. "I'd be upset by any student who's this bad."

"You don't know anything about her."

"I know all I need to know."

"Hell you do. She used to be on hard drugs. You know what saved her?—an education. She was a heroin addict, and she went cold turkey, and that was three years ago. You got any idea what it's like to get that haint off your back and keep it off?"

"I don't see what—"

"No, you wouldn't. She knows what it's like for kids today. She knows the streets. She knows drugs, crime, prostitution, poverty, living on welfare, early pregnancy, incest—she knows more about real life than you'll ever know, boy."

Struggling to maintain control of himself, Laxalt shoves Victorene's paper into his briefcase. "Then let her be a counselor or something. She has no business in the classroom."

"Classroom's exactly where she'll do the most good."

"No, the most harm."

Easter tilts his head. "How come you got it in for her? She give you some lip?"

"She didn't do anything. She's a terrible student, that's all, and she'd be even worse as a teacher."

"You think when you come to a university you won't find as much as you do out there." The drop in the abrasive volume of Easter's voice catches Laxalt's attention and makes him turn at the door. Easter is stroking his peacock tuft of hair. "It's no different," he continues dispiritedly. "You find it anyway."

Laxalt flushes and bites his lip. "We have to have standards—we must."

"Ya, lily white standards."

Laxalt throws up his hands. "That's not fair. Standards don't have any color."

Easter snorts as he walks around behind his desk. "They don't huh." He sits down, turns a folder, and begins to read.

"Jesus," Laxalt says.

Easter does not look up.

As Laxalt leaves the School of Education building, his mind a-whirl, he denies to himself again and again that he is driven by any sense of personal vengeance or racial superiority. He does not hold anything against blacks. But he does, he does, and he knows it. He runs through a white litany of slurs against them. It's normal, it's natural to have such feelings, he tells himself. The February sun is failing to warm his chilled bones. As brittle leaves blow across the path where he walks back to his office he mutters to himself, I'm not a bigot, I'm not, I'm not.

Second papers have come in from his Critical Approaches to Literature course, and Laxalt sits at his desk brooding over the first page of Victorene Jenkins' work. Two weeks before, he focused on the principles of historical and sociocultural criticism. Laxalt feels that his lectures on *The Crucible* were inspired. In the zeal of his newly declared war against prejudice, they became passionately motivated exhortations to avoid character assassination, systematized conformity, corporate hysteria. He lifted all of his ideas from earlier critics but now considers them his own. He reassures himself that he is capable of judging Victorene fairly. And even if he were prejudiced in some slight way, it isn't against color, he tells himself, it's against stupidity, stupidity like this. Chin cupped in his hand, he rereads the first part of Victorene's paper:

> No one actualy seen it but but him. that caused so
> much pain for so many innicent peo/ple.
> I think that author Miller is really trying to show

how viscious and under handed means that McCarthy
ism deplicted. It seems to that Miller displays Mc
  Carthyism on the same level as a womans skorn , it
is just as sinceless. Abigail had been defeated, just
    has was McCarthy was conquered. in order to
possible gain personal goals. Though the play was
not truely the factual accounts.

Laxalt puts his head in his hands. What can be done in
a case like this? It extends beyond illiteracy. It reflects a
condition that is hopeless. It belongs in his hopeless file.
He goes down the hall into the department copier room and
xeroxes the two pages before marking them. Back in his
office he flips through folders in a file, working backward
from WRITING: SUPERIOR, WRITING: PLAGIARISM,
to WRITING: HOPELESS. He pulls out the folder, puts
Victorene's on top of the stack, and starts to put it away.
He stops and, instead, returns to his desk and begins leafing
through the folder, filled with copies of papers he has
received and others that are accompanied by notes from
friends teaching elsewhere in the state and around the
country. The first is from Max Parsons at a four-year
college in Utah. His memo begins, "Here's a piece of one
student's response from an in-class writing assignment."

I think the worst book I have read has been the Great
Gatsby and I dont know who wrought it (they ought
to be shoot) and unless I was missing a few pages
(and I was not) that should have told me at least
what the book was about. It went completly over my
head. The book made no sense at all whatsoever.
It did'nt tell you who was narating what it was at
least about and as far as I am conserned it did'nt
even have a plot which I could indentify with the
book. I myself would be ashamed to put such a lousy
piece of workmanship on the news stand. If author

could have given the people some names and reasons
why the people should even be in the book then
maybe I could go back and read the book, but until
the book is not rewritten I refuse even to look at the
cover.

Laxalt chuckles at Max's parting shot: "I knew this
critique would make your day. Pass on these comments to
Fitzgerald; I'm sure he's worried about his readership in
Utah. If he doesn't improve that book, they're sure to take
it off the newstands here."

He flips to a batch from Norm Gottlieb, teaching at a
JC in northern California. Scrawled at the top: "This is
what we get every day."

The deer and the fish lives completely different
well as there shape and size. The fish has to live in
water. As where the deer on the country side. The
fish has gill to help breath. The deer has a nose in
which they breath.The food they eat are not the
same. The fish eat bugs and smaller fish. The deer
eats different kinds of plant life. The size of a fish
comes in different sizes. From as little as a minow
and as big as a wale. The deer stands about fore
or five tall. The mail deer will grow a set of horns
where the fish won't. The fish has a wet slipperly
serfish where as the deer has a coat of fear. Both or
nice to hunt and fish.

He flips through a few others, reading a sentence here,
a sentence there: "Refugees are clusting into this country
by the thousands. Speaking no english and understanding
no english. Taking job from employeed mmnorities that
have been here going through think and thin, in order to
get that low paying good job. In which will be depride
from them cause of this scared to revolt against there

dictatorship regimes I stress to you that know one, should be aloud to work in this country with united state citizenship" . . . "The cartoon character Bugs Bunney has the nack of getting in trouble when he has to. Alot of times. I wish I was bugs becaus I would like to get out of trouble more often to. Bugs Bunney has the power that most people would like to have" . . . "Helan portraits a woman that hates the Chines because of the war and hates living there" . . . "I just finished bathing my baby when I put her clothes on, she was 10 months old at the time."

Hands behind his head, he stares at his book lined wall. Language incompetence has become a disease. It isn't just in need of cosmetic repair, fixing the occasional laugh-producing faux pas of a student: *gorilla* for *guerrilla* or *granite* for *granted*, *crucifiction* for *crucifixion* or *jeans* for *genes*. To the contrary, it is nationwide, infesting government, the military, business, and, worst of all, education. He glances at a note to the side of his desk, kept there for the past month to feed his pain. It is a memo to the staff from one of the secretaries. He has scrawled across the top: FOR CHRISTSAKE, CAN YOU BELIEVE THIS IS A COLLEGE-EDUCATED, EXPERIENCED, ENGLISH DEPARTMENT SECRETARY! It reads:

> After Registration Dennis Yerblans stated, that
> these who had come to sign in oult be allowed in
> first, I have the original sign in sheets. When
> you find notes in your box that someone has been
> added, that means that I have checked the original
> sheet and have found that there is room. If you
> have any questions tommorow when classes begin-if
> students tell you they have been registered in-
> please have them check with me before allowing
> theminto class if you have more than one who wants
> in, as we have waiting lists for several classes.

Laxalt is by now leaning so far backwards in his chair that it nearly tips over. He expels his breath and closes the folder decisively. Annie would tell him he's being a terrible snob. She's good at reminding him to guard against the snobbism inherent in his role of advantage. Of course students make silly stupid mistakes. English professors love to chortle over them. But surely these gaffes are trivial. She has a point. Life consists of far more important matters. The great sprawling country of which he's so proud was not built by people who fussed over the niceties of language. After all, he himself had grown up on the broken accent, the mangled sentences of his own grand-father. What did it matter whether *HAIR-us* was preferred over *Ha-RASS* to a Scandahoovian who worked with his hands for sixty years? But making cabinets is far different from working with young minds in a school, as Victorene Jenkins would be doing.

"I've got to talk to her," he mutters. "This charade can't go on."

"Let your boy sit outside so we can concentrate," Laxalt says. "I've got some art books over there he can look at."

"He be fine where he is."

Laxalt sighs. "Did you bring the paper I marked?"

"Ain't no grade on it."

"I couldn't grade it—I want it redone." In the long run rewriting won't do her any good and he knows it. He can't bring himself to tell her what he's thinking. He wants to appear fair, although his mind is still made up that she will fail his course. He continues: "If I had graded it, it would have been a flat *F*. You don't want an *F* on the paper, do you?"

She looks at him, her face impassive, and says nothing. This time, instead of filling in, he waits for a response from her. She takes out the silence on her son by telling him to shut up. "Hold on now," Laxalt says. "He wasn't doing anything." Laxalt feels his voice rising. "I want you to talk to me. Don't keep using him as an excuse." He tries to ignore her pout. They glare at one another until she drops her eyes. "Victorene, are you sure you?—" Laxalt lowers his voice. "I still don't understand why you chose English. There are other things you could do."

She shifts in her seat. "You tryin to tell me I can't be no teacher."

"Explain to me what's so important about teaching." He waits. "I said, explain to me what's so important about teaching." He waits. "Well."

"'S a good job. I likes chirren."

"Is that all?"

"I likes talkin 'bout things in books. Makes me feel like I'm doing some real good."

"What *things*?"

"Same's you talk 'bout."

"Oh, you can do that, huh. Tell me what you'd say." He sits back waiting. She stares at the point near his desk that she always fixes upon when in his office. He slides his chair over to it. She twists her head away. He smirks as he slides back behind his desk. "I think we better change the subject, don't you?" A long minute passes as he seeks something to talk about. "You must've been influenced by some good teachers when you were young. Role models. Who were they?" He waits. "Did you have any?"

"One. Mrs. Jefferson."

"Why was she so good?"

"She talked lots. Kidded around. Wasn't nothin she wouldn't talk about. Used to talk to her 'bout—'bout girl stuff. Didn't have no mother to talk to—she out sleepin 'round, my dad in jail."

"Oh, what for?"

She scowls at him.

"It's all right, you don't have to tell me."

"Killed two men who was cheatin him at cards."

"Good heavens."

"Don't make no never mind. Ain't seen him in seven years."

"You had this Mrs. Jefferson for English?"

"Yup. Two years in a row."

"She didn't teach you anything, Victorene. You may have liked her and admired her, but you didn't learn one damn thing from her."

"Did too. Got *A*s from her. Got *A*s from Mr. Hobart, too. You won't even give me no grade."

"Grades don't matter that much. What counts is whether you can handle the language. And I'm afraid you can't— you're way behind where you should be."

"Ain't either. I be catching up. I'm goin to do real good in this course."

Laxalt pinches his eyes with thumb and forefinger, then shakes his head. "You need to back up and start remedial English." He takes a deep breath and exhales slowly. "You're going to have a tough time getting through my course. You may not make it." Why is he still unable to tell her directly that she's going to fail?

Panic sweeps over her face anyway. "I got to have this course. You goin to stop me from graduating. You can't do that."

"Yes I can. Both of your papers have been—I can fail you on writing alone. I'll know definitely next week after your first exam."

She fights against the fear that crinkles her forehead and glazes her eyes. "I'm goin to do good in that exam. Real good."

Her score turns out to be 65, a *D+*, by no means the abysmal failure he expected. Her essays, though miserably written, are not without some ideas, and she does better than he thinks she could in the objective section and in identification and discussion of quotations. He can make some adjustments in the exam to lower her grade, yet he's afraid to do it. He wants an outright failure of the exam as evidence to show the School of Education that her case is hopeless. The object would be to deny her the possibility of going any farther in pursuit of a credential. Now he isn't sure what to do. If only her status were as clear-cut as it is for her friend Naomi Gaines. He ran into Naomi that afternoon in the hall and asked her to stop by his office.

Her appearance makes him smile with pleasure, although her flat nose, large jaw, protruding eyes, corn-rowed hair hardly make her an attractive women. He likes her looks for a particular reason. Once in a while as a hobby he restores old pieces of furniture. She puts him in mind of fine wood. Her skin is as flawless as highly polished black walnut. Her large strong teeth give her a dazzling smile—and she smiles often. She sits straight backed opposite him, looking him square in the eye, perfectly at ease.

"Naomi, I called you in because I want your help. You're an honor student and you'll go on to become a very good teacher. How do you feel about blacks who aren't as good as you, who can't write, who don't speak well? Do you think they should become teachers?"

"You're talking about Victorene."

Laxalt colors. "Umm. Yes and no. I say no because I'm

concerned with a bigger problem. It goes beyond one person—you know that."

"Yes sir, I do." She grows pensive. "I don't know how to answer."

"Try, please. I want to know how you truly feel."

"You talked one day in class about the head-heart conflict. I'm torn in the same way. Intellectually I get mad at folks like Victorene or Rufer Jones or Willie Spitz on the football team. They don't try in academics. Sometimes I also think they're plain dumb. Then my heart jumps up and says, whoa, hold it right there. Look at the families they come from, the rotten schooling they got, all the disadvantages they had. Sure they're at fault, but only partially. That's why I'm so torn." She gives him a sideways look. "I'm not being fair—I said Victorene didn't try, but she's studying harder'n I've ever seen her study for your class."

"You've been helping her, haven't you? You helped her with the exam."

"We studied together. That's okay, isn't it?"

"Of course. Some of the best learning of all goes on when students help each other."

"Doctor Laxalt, I—" Naomi hesitates. "She knows you don't like her."

"I don't dislike her."

"The class is very important to her. She says her whole life depends on this class."

"No need for her to be so dramatic." He swivels in his chair. "Let me put a harder question to you. Would you let someone like Victorene teach your own children? Would you want her to teach them English?"

"Oh my."

"Come on."

"Well, the part of me that's her friend, the part of me that makes us blacks together, they make me say, yes, put her in the classroom. The part of me that's a teacher says, no way."

Laxalt comes around his desk and bends to Naomi. He wants to give her a hug. Instead he takes her hand. "Thanks for being honest." He straightens. "Been a long day. Let me walk you out."

On the way home Frank stops at a discount liquor mart to buy some wine, the emblem of a secret language between him and his wife, signal of a private time later that night. He makes sure as he goes by the check stands to leaf through latest copies of *Penthouse* and *Oui*. Not that he needs to be inspired—he's horny enough. He rationalizes away his guilty pleasure by masking it as curiosity. He peers down at *Hustler*, wanting to rip off the plastic seal—but he never has.

It's all right to let images of vaginas and breasts fill his head, he tells himself. His marriage is secure, comfortable. He and Annie have a good relationship, if he overlooks her tendency to mother him. Except at times of passion, they rarely speak of love. They enjoy each other's company and get along well. They love their children dearly. Their marriage suffers little from the weight of stored grievances or anxieties. They're neither brown baggers nor disaster seekers. Having discovered that they do not qualify for those terms and others like them, they have set aside the advice book on marriage from which they've learned them, and it hasn't been taken from its shelf for nine years. A wave of good feeling passes through Frank: he's a good husband and a good father.

His good feeling fights against another quite different one. He has bought the wine to assuage guilt. For the past week or so, as he put the final touches on a paper to be delivered at a conference in Los Angeles, he was obsessed with thoughts of a former student of his: Courtney Raines. Courtney Raines, who had taken four classes from him. Courtney Raines: his favorite student over eleven years of teaching, the only one who had ever got to him. He had seen her develop from a big-eyed quiet frosh to a cool, self-assured senior, and a stunning one at that: shoulder-length wheat hair, long slender legs, full breasts. He never laid a hand on her, each year congratulating himself for not doing it when fervently he wanted to.

He knows that a few of his colleagues have seduced some of their students, males and females. All such liaisons he considers unprofessional, beneath him. He has made up his mind—or so he told himself years before—that he will always remain professional, and that means no harrassment, no innuendoes, no pressures, no forced intimacies. And yet Courtney Raines got to him. Although he sensed that she wanted him, he continued to refrain from so much as touching her. Professionalism, he told himself. Down deep he knew what really prevented him from doing what he wanted to do, and professionalism had nothing to do with it. It was fear. Fear of rejection. Fear of embarrassment. Fear of fear.

So she graduated and went off to southern California to work in an advertising agency. His star, his budding poet, his neophyte literary critic, whom he wanted to go on for M.A. and Ph.D., and come back and teach alongside him, was now pushing bras or booze or whatever hucksterism had compelled her to sell herself to. How many boyfriends did she have? Or had she married? He didn't know. Since her departure he had longed to write her, to phone her, but he did nothing. Professionalism, he told himself. And yet often in his dreams they made love in the most erotic ways. His fantasies of a life with her magnified or receded, depending upon his mood and circumstances.

He buys the wine for a third reason, juxtaposed against his guilt: an exuberant overpowering feeling of machismo. That afternoon from his office, heart pounding, throat dry, he called Courtney Raines to tell her that he would be in Los Angeles for a three-day conference—could he see her while he was there? She would be thrilled at the prospect. That was her very word: thrilled.

When his wife kisses him at the airport upon his return, Frank draws back in pain. His upper lip is puffed where Courtney had bit him. "What is it?" his wife says, "what happened?" Averting his eyes, he replies, "Cold sore."

The class is arguing over Henry James. Having completed work on formalism, Laxalt has assigned the short novel *The Turn of the Screw* as an introduction to psychological criticism. He has summarized Edmund Wilson's psychoanalytical reading of the governess and now has opened up the discussion with the old chestnut: which way to interpret, as a literal ghost story or as an imaginative projection of the psyche of a frustrated spinster?

The Compulsives dominate at the beginning as they always do. Slaughter starts by arguing for the acceptance of a literal ghost story and cites Coleridge's remark on the temporary suspension of disbelief as supporting evidence. "If you accept the ghost of Hamlet's father, then you accept the presence of Quint and Miss Jessel. It has to be a ghost story." He sits back, arms folded, absolutely certain of his position.

Hauptmann leaps in. "Besides, James himself referred to it as his '*amusette*, a piece of ingenuity'—it was about 'demon spirits,' if not ghosts per se." Hauptmann waves his intelligence around like pendants in the vanguard of a marching band. When he goes on to argue that James didn't intend the work to be taken seriously, Laxalt sees an opportunity to explain the intentional fallacy. But Hauptmann persists over the beginning of his definition. These are the times when Laxalt wonders about helping Hauptmann get into graduate school. He's a likely prospect, if only he weren't so arrogant. "There's no way you can read the Preface and his letters and conclude it's anything else but a story about ghosts," Hauptmann says flatly. "Okay, now let me get back to intentional fallacy," Laxalt says. When he's finished he looks back to Hauptmann. "So you see, Kurt, it's quite possible to have an interpretation different from what the writer may have expressed or intended. Robert Frost said one time that a poet is entitled to whatever may be found in his poem. He's right, you know. You can't make up stuff; you have to be able to support an interpretation within the context of the work itself, but various interpretations are possible. Do you see?" Hauptmann gives a slight nod, but the pugilistic thrust of his chin asserts, Who else to trust but the writer; after all, he wrote it.

Fey's dulcet voice comes from near the window. "I support what you first suggested, Dr. Laxalt: everything exists in the governess's head. Why else would you assign the story under 'Psychological Criticism'?" After laughter of the class subsides, she lists her reasons. They show that she has read Wilson and others supporting him. She has marked a half-dozen citations in the text to support her ideas. Hauptmann and Slaughter counter argue. An Occasional slips in a remark, and then another. Laxalt always likes this time of class discussion when the Compulsives lose their stranglehold and the Occasionals take over. He always hopes to hear from the Mutes, but only rarely do they ever break out of their self-protective shells. He keeps himself quiet and enjoys the give-and-take among the students. The argument ricochets for another ten or fifteen minutes: pro ghost story, pro repressed spinster. Laxalt grows heady over his superior teaching abilities. He has every reason to be proud, he assures himself, for here is professionalism at its best. To his delight, a Mute speaks up. Laxalt is gentle with her, even though her reasoning about Mrs. Grose is faulty. After all, with such encouragement, the Mute might become an Occasional. The students continue arguing.

Laxalt's gaze roams the class, passes Naomi Gaines, passes Sjaan Mermeer-Egan, alights on Victorene Jenkins, who sits near the door, for once without her son beside her. When Laxalt sees Victorene shift on her buttocks he knows she's going to blurt out something. She's an Occasional, but rather than ever raise her hand in a discussion she merely begins talking, sometimes over another voice. Her opinions—often non sequiturs—are rendered with a fierce glare upon the instructor. At a slight lull, she begins:

"You was talkin yestiday 'bout the lil girl, you know, the other day, puttin a stick in the little hole. You know, this piece of wood like a boat, screwing it in. Phall—sumpin, whatever, you know, you was sayin like it was, I mean, having sex, you know. Well, it ain't got nothing to do with sex. It's like she's stabbin the gubness right in the heart. It's like voodoo, you know, like she's stickin pins in her to kill her."

A titter comes from one side of the room, then another, and Laxalt sees eyeballs rolling. A silence settles over the class. How cruel they are, he thinks, the way they put her down. He wants to spring to her defense, but what can he say to support such an asinine interpretation.

"Well, we're all entitled to our opinions," he says, "but, remember, you have to be able to provide support within the context of the work. There's no evidence in the story to support this reading, Victorene."

"'Smy interprashun," Victorene says. "You say different interprashuns is, you know, you can have different interprashuns."

"Yes, I did say so, but that doesn't mean you can interpret in some fanciful way. What you're doing is symbol hunting." Laxalt enumerates its dangers. She isn't understanding a word he says. When he turns to her once more, she repeats, "Well, 'smy interprashun."

Laxalt tries to get a discussion going again, to no avail. Class debate is delicately buoyant—the exchange between him and the black woman has deflated it. For the remaining few minutes of the class, Laxalt must return to his lecture notes.

As Frank stands outside by the entryway flowerboxes, letting a fine spray play over the azalea, the sacroccoa, the marigolds in between, down to the lobelia, celosia, pansies, impatiens, Darwinian tulips, his thoughts are on Victorene. She has failed in her third straight paper and a recent quiz, and keeps on making a fool of herself in class. She continues to drag along her son wherever she goes. He wears the same sport coat, same hat, same trousers, same tie—only his shirt seems different once in a while. And the child wears the same wide-eyed look he had the first day he appeared in class alongside his mother. Kite Tailing and Other Irrational Acts. The Easter break is coming, and Frank needs to make a decision about the woman.

He knows what his colleagues would do. Feed her to the lions. 37 to 2. The thumbs-uppers are a couple of softies in the writing program, notorious as easy graders, especially of minority students. Brainwashed by the liberalism of an earlier generation, they have grown old believing that special privileges must be accorded the disadvantaged. The rest have leaped up on the ramparts of higher standards, determined now to stem the rising tide of mediocrity.

If it's so easy for thirty-seven others to turn thumbs down, then why not him? Why can't he finish her off and stop being so preoccupied with her? He likes to think that while he's strong and forthright he's also more sensitive and humane than his colleagues. Why, it's simply not in his nature to be hardhearted. Think of the obstacles Victorene has had to overcome. One can't expect a foreign student to achieve mastery of a new language. Victorene is in a similar boat—standard English is alien to her. But there's the rub: she's going to teach it. What would his neighbors do, he wonders, were they faced by the prospect of having Victorene teach their children?

The hardest on her would probably be the Arbuthnots, the only blacks on the block. Frank glances catty-corner across the street at their brick-front frame house. When Arbuthnot bought the house three years before (at a price fifteen thousand dollars more than it was worth), some neighbors were incensed. One early morning when Frank got up to run, he saw a cross on the Arbuthnot's lawn. It was made of crudely nailed pieces of old 2x4, strewn under it matches and bits of charred paper, obviously the work of children. Frank was outraged and deliberated whether to remove the cross. He was afraid that if he went near it he would be seen as the perpetrator. But he steeled himself, strode onto the lawn, snatched up the cross, and threw it in his car. On the way to the park he tossed it in a dumpster that sat at the front of a house undergoing repair. He was deeply ashamed of his neighbors.

Although he couldn't pinpoint the guilty, he guessed that a couple of the Gridley boys were responsible. They live two houses over on the corner behind motorcycles and cars parked on dead-dry grass. Their crude, big-breasted mother thrives on trivial hard feelings that give her meaningless life meaning. A divorcée, she has taken in a lover the age of her oldest son. Along with another two girls in the family, the place crawls with dogs and cats. It's a lively bastion of seediness and pot and rock: nigger-hating, spic-hating, kike-hating, intellect-hating, hating whatever it doesn't understand, which is almost everything. So Frank knows well how Victorene would fare at their hands: they don't care if she's a lousy potential teacher; they'd lynch her for being black.

Directly across the street, shades always drawn behind barred windows, lives a retired couple, one a diabetic, the other with an ulcerated leg. Whenever either manages to emerge outside, released temporarily from the Cyclopean eye of a front-room TV, it is to bemoan what's happening to the neighborhood: their fear of transient families and blacks and chicanos and Vietnamese; alarm at the increase in muggings, vandalism, wife beatings, rapes, household robberies; bafflement that their beloved old city is corroding as insidiously as rust. Then, following resigned sigh, back to join life's partner in the inner sanctum of their illnesses, their soap operas, their game shows. They have no children to suffer—Victorene means nothing to them as long as she stays out of their neighborhood.

But next door children would suffer, and opposition can be counted on from Sarah Picardy, who had once been a high-stepping drum majorette for minority causes. Unable to find a job teaching, she has gone to work for the Department of Public Assistance at a branch office in a black ghetto. After six years there she has turned into a cynical, hardened bigot. Surrounded daily by black smells and black cries and black hate, she cannot bear the utter dependence of her clients on the welfare system while at the same time they seethe with anger against it. Her loud voice piercing through the walls from next door reflects her frustration: she dumps on her husband as she herself is dumped on day after day by the poor and the greedy. She takes pains in relating to Frank their venom: "You honky, when I gwine git my money, mine, mine, what due to me" . . . "How you 'spect me to feed my fambly, when this here what we got, right chere, foateen cents, and ain but the middle of the month" . . . "That mothahfuckah done split, and you sits here and tells me I cain't get no more bread. Shit, shit on him, and shit on you you mothafuckin white bitch." Because she can never talk back to her clients, her only recourse (aside from quitting, which she will never consider in view of her high salary) is to store up her bitterness for release at home. In that household Victorene wouldn't stand a chance except maybe with Larry, Larry the carpet layer, Larry the linoleum layer, Larry the lady layer, who has turned into a chaser because he can't stand being dumped on all the time.

Frank turns to water the other side. How would Victorene fare to starboard? Worse than to port because Lucky Doler can hate more. He's a specialist in dumping on his wife Sue and their two boys, born thirteen years apart, the latter conceived out of desperation to hold together an already shaky marriage. Lucky works for a contractor who specializes in custom-made homes built for an elite clientele in exclusive northerly sites perched on hills or poised over the Winding River. So, unlike Sarah facing the poor, Lucky deals with the highest rung of the economic ladder: corporate executives and wheelerdealer businessmen, incorporated MDs and dentists. Day after day he's dumped on by them and by their wives: "The light switch was supposed to be bronze, not brass, and what's it doing there when it was supposed to be an inch this way" . . . "You

see that flaw in the dormer casement—replace it, pronto"
. . . "No flunky is going to con me. What do you think
we're paying a half-million for?—junk. I want it fixed
now, and that means now." So he comes home and dumps
on his wife. And she dumps on the seventeen-year old who
takes it out on the little kid who gives it to the dog. As the
voices rise on both sides, Frank retreats into the house and
pours himself a drink.

When he comes back outside to put away the hose, he
sees George Arbuthnot out watering his plants and waves
at him. At first, George does not see him. He's scowling
upward at the wing of a new thirty-unit stucco apartment
building that leers into his bedrooms. He and his wife, a
lovely mulatto, have fought hard against its construction.
They remonstrated against the city council and the city
planning commission, without success. But the petition
drive they spearheaded led to a rezoning that prevents the
encroachment of additional apartment projects in the
neighborhood. Meantime they can do nothing about this
monstrosity. The bottles and cans littering its parking lot
disgust them. Its squealing tires worry them everytime their
three small children play outside. Its cacophonous music
ruins their sleep. And George personally holds in scorn
every black who has moved into it.

How will he feel when his children grow older and are
greeted by Victorene in a classroom? Frank crosses the
street, and, after explaining, puts the question to him
directly. Arbuthnot tilts his large-nostriled nose backward
and laughs. "You're asking me, would you have your kid
operated on by a surgeon who can't cut?"

"But we need minority teachers."

"Sure we do, same as CPAs, bankers, engineers, you
name it. But lots of black folks got the idea they don't need
to work hard to get where they're going. They just want to

be there, whether they're trained or not. Well, I don't buy it. I worked my ass off to be a CPA. I expect others to do the same. Your girl wants the easy way, without paying any price."

"She may be willing to pay a price—she has a fixation about teaching. I'm afraid she hasn't got what it takes."

"That's why *you* are in the position you're in. It's your job to keep out the duds. If she's not qualified she's not qualified, period."

"But she's black, and I don't want to hurt her."

Arbuthnot gives him a long look. "The way you didn't want to hurt me."

"I don't know what you mean."

George watches the spray shooting in a rainbow arch across his curb strip. "The cross you took off my lawn a couple years ago. Yes, I saw you."

"Why didn't you ever say anything?"

"Never any need to, until now. One way, it was good of you to do it—not so good in another. We had to learn ourselves to cope with the prejudice around here."

"Hasn't it dissipated by now?"

"Sure, some." George turns the spray to the trellises alongside his house. "Don't forget mine either. I don't like most whites. And I don't like my own kind: welfare niggers pouring in next door, this woman you're telling me about, all the rest like 'em. You're not doing this Victorene any favor by overlooking her incompetence."

By the time Frank reaches the middle of the street between Arbuthnot's home and his own, he has made a decision.

Victorene stands before Laxalt's desk, shaking. "Why for you do me this?" Her fury has turned her lips gray.

"What?" He knows exactly what she means.

"You know what I say, you call the man, Dean what's-his-name, you talk to people over in the school. You tell 'em I's no good, I can't be no teacher, what for you do that?"

"Sit down, please. Have your boy wait out there."

"He go where I goes."

"No, I won't talk to you this way. Let him wait outside."

"Now you tryin to bust up me and my Thal."

"I'm not trying to do any such—" When she grabs the boy's hand and starts out the door, he raises his voice. "Stop it. Get back in here."

She turns. Her eyes are crazed. She pushes the boy toward the corner of the room where he cowers, hands behind him. For a moment Laxalt fears that she might have a knife or a razor on her. "You fuck me over," she says, teeth clenched, bending toward Laxalt over his desk. "You show that Dean all my stuff. Make me look real bad. They has a meeting. He tell me I can't be in their program no more." She straightens and lets out a great shrieking moan.

"Calm down," Laxalt says. He waits for her to regain her composure. Her son has put his hands over his face and is watching her through his opened fingers. "This isn't the end of the world," Laxalt continues. "You can do other things. Maybe you can learn how to be a counselor. From what Easter tells me you'd be good at it."

"Don't want to do nothin else but teach."

"Don't you understand?—you can't. The deprived leading the deprived. You'd only hurt them more. One thing sure: you'd never be able to pass the CBEST. I know the criteria, I know why you'd fail. Your writing is disorganized, it lacks focus, you don't know how to develop ideas, your writing is confused and contradictory, and, my god, you make countless mistakes in grammar and mechanics and spelling."

"What you tellin me about that CBEST for? That ain't for a time. The semester ain't even up. You didn't give me no chance to finish the course."

"You were going to fail anyway. I was only trying to spare you. I have to fail you. I have no choice."

"You spittin on me. You spittin on me cause I'm black. Black and poor."

"Victorene, please." From his angle below her, he can see the taut cords on either side of her neck.

"You think I'm dumb, but I ain't."

Laxalt closes his eyes and then looks up at her again. A sheen comes into her eyes, glistening brightly, but the face below is shattered.

"You got no call to do me bad. I never done nothin to you, never, nothin."

She spins and runs from the office, leaving her wide-eyed boy behind. Laxalt and the boy look at each other wordlessly. Then, hands in his pockets, head down, the boy shuffles out to try to find his mother.

Over the Easter break Courtney flies up for a weekend in San Francisco. She takes a suite at the Hyatt Regency on the Embarcadaro. Frank has to make up an elaborate excuse to his wife about the necessity for going off to conduct research in Berkeley. The weekend costs him nine hundred dollars. He doesn't know how he can get away with it. He feels himself slipping into a quagmire.

"Dr. Easter from the School of Ed is here," the secretary says on the inter-office phone. "Can he see you?"

"Sure," Laxalt says. He stares out the office window. The campus is in glorious full color. A couple more weeks and the semester will be over. So will his triumph over the adversity of a semester with clinkers like Victorene Jenkins and her ilk. Good riddance, he tells himself.

Easter bristles into the office. "I hope you're satisfied with what you done."

Laxalt stares at him.

"Well, don'tchu want to know?"

"You'll tell me, whether I want you to or not."

"Victorene Jenkins, she's dead."

"No. How?"

"OD."

"Oh God. When?"

"Easter day. Had enough heroin in her to kill a team of horses."

"How awful. And the boy?"

Easter runs his fingers through his tuft of hair. "What boy?"

"Her boy. Is he okay?"

"Don't know nothing about a boy. What you trying to do?—throw off your blame on something else. You killed that woman, sure's I'm standing here."

When Easter has finally stopped sputtering and leaves, Laxalt's thoughts turn more to the son than to the dead woman. The poor little surviving child. No mother, father who knows?—a bum, a criminal, a heroin addict. What will happen to the boy? Poor tyke. But he can be saved— the solution is clear. How noble. The child can be adopted. Why yes, how kind. We'll raise him. Everybody will say of Frank Laxalt, now there is a decent, generous human being, takes in that poor little colored kid, a homeless waif, right into his own home, gives him the best of everything, makes him what he is to become: a doctor, a senator, a professor.

Five minutes later, Frank's heart is not so open. What about the effects of a new child in the house, and a black one at that? How will he be accepted by his own children? What if the kid turns out to be rotten?

By the time he has put to himself a dozen more of these questions, his altruism begins to fade. By the next morning, without ever speaking to his wife, he has talked himself out of the idea, having dredged up every possible objection. The gesture is, he decides finally, impossible. He has no idea what will happen to the boy.

He becomes very occupied for a few months with his own children.

"How was school?"

"Okay."

"Like your new teachers?"

"Yeah, I guess so."

"You don't seem so sure."

"They're okay, 'cept for one. In social studies." Evi peers up at her father. "He's a black man."

"That's nice. Who is he?"

"Mr. Willson. Two *l*s. He goes, 'And don't you let me see no one *l*.'"

"*Says, says*, for the millionth time. Not *goes*. What else did he say?"

"He goes, 'Children, I'm gonna learn you good.' Daddy, it's *teach*, I know it's *teach*."

SLIDES

In an apartment the size of a ball field in Pacific Heights, the mother comes with a white slide tray invaded by her bosom. She's a big woman, firm and supple, like a boa constrictor, with lavender eyes, who wisely has never dyed her hair. "Bring me a drink, Chan," she calls and, turning to me, pats a seat beside her.

"Mother, do you have to," Mavis says to her.

"I can't think of anything more a crashing bore," Channing Cosgrove says from the bar.

"We're going out on the terrace," Mavis says. "Come on, Teddie, bring our drinks."

A mulatto maid carries in a slide machine and tacks away on the sea of carpet.

Channing Cosgrove serves his wife her drink and, carrying the decanter with him, follows Ted and Mavis to the terrace.

The mother watches them. "She's just a little bit too tall for Teddie, isn't she?"

"He's six feet," I say.

"It's those heels, I suppose. Well, now. Flip the light there." The beam drills a blank eye into the wall. She clicks the machine with her right hand. Her thigh presses against mine. From infant to dark eyed, dark faced nymph, her daughter Mavis flips by me through a lush fairyland.

"Yes, that's when we were in Ankara . . . Baghdad . . . Damascus there . . . Tehràn . . . Cyprus."

In the Damascus phase, behind the mother and the hand-held knee-high child squinting in the sunlight stands a lean young man in a white coat. The backdrop of a white scolloped wall accentuates his dark eyes and the darkish cast of his skin. A proud smile is fixed on his sensual and rather cruel mouth.

"He looks enough like Mavis to be her brother," I say, half an ear on the laughter of Mavis and Channing Cosgrove from the terrace.

"Our houseboy Raoul," she says. "The usual raffish, undependable sort. Oh, he did stay on for awhile, though, even after poor Dawson's death. I don't know whatever happened to him. He went off to fight in a war of some sort." A spearpoint of fingernail pierces into the beam. "That's Mavis's father. Poor Dawson."

Poor Dawson stays a continuous blur: out of focus, or face shadowed by a silly sun helmet, or lost in the distance at the base of a minaret.

"We were eating dinner at the time. I was just having my wine—Raoul knew so many marvelous wines. Poor Dawson didn't even get to finish his. I heard him gasp. He grabbed hold of his throat, turned quite purple, and fell with his head right in the eggplant. How horrid. He was only forty-something, sound as a dollar, but you know what can happen to a man's heart sometimes. You're not even listening to me." Her thigh presses harder into mine. "Don't worry—you won't miss a thing out there."

"Oh no, I'm listening," I say.

From a mound of flowers on poor Dawson's bier in the foreground of a bleak New England landscape and from a flag at half-mast over one of his liquor distilleries, the slides become the flipping pages of a European travel folder: the Riviera, Paris, London, the ski slopes of Switzerland. Two other fathers, a dozen schools and colleges, and uncounted airplane trips later, Mrs. Cosgrove comes to the final slide.

"The wedding will be a whole new tray," she adds, rising. "Here, come look at my masterpiece." Her eyes glitter in the semidarkness. "Yes, the light."

I follow her past a mosaic coffee table as long as a diving board. On a corner wall hangs an oil portrait of a girl about seventeen. I want to say, "Who is it?" but I don't because I know. Nevertheless, any resemblance between Mavis and the celestial being draped in white chiffon in the portrait is nearly coincidental.

"No one knew how to capture her true spirit except Chan. It was his first commission. Now you see why he's the most sought-after portrait painter we have."

I must wend around a white grand piano to look at the portrait up close. Its eyes follow me every step of the way.

"Lovely," I say.

"Teddie will settle her down, won't he?"

"Sure he will," I say.

"Well, if he won't, Teddie's father will."

"How do you mean?"

"Well, you know they wanted to live together, and his father said, 'no legal wife, no legal junior partnership.' You didn't know that? Teddie said you were his best friend at Boalt Hall."

"He didn't tell me."

"Why didn't you bring your young lady with you? Mavis said you were doubling tonight."

"Yes, later, when she gets off work."

"Oh yes." Her voice drops between the 'oh' and 'yes.' "She's a receptionist, or something, isn't she?"

"A nurse," I say. "We're saving up to get married."

"Isn't that nice. Before Mavis's?"

"I have to pass the Bar first."

"But of course you will. Both of you." She fixes upon me the critical eye of a tailor. "Have you met Mavis's friend DeDe Courtlander? You've heard of the Courtlanders?"

"Who hasn't," I say.

"Delightful girl. She and Mavis are just like that. She flew down to Mexico to dump Bobbie Vanderhuis. Would you like to meet her? She'll be back any day now."

"I don't know, I—"

Mavis comes in. "She's finished with those stupid slides. Let's go."

In the foyer Mrs. Cosgrove smiles at her daughter. "Not too late, darling. You have your sitting early tomorrow, remember. We must get pictures to the newspapers."

"Damn, I forgot," Mavis says.

On the way down the elevator, Ted outlines a change in plans. He and Mavis are going to a motel first. They'll stop by my girl's house maybe later. Over the Bay Bridge, Ted whips back and forth across lanes in the Porsche that the Cosgroves have given to Mavis as an engagement present.

"Well, what does the Stockton farm boy think of them?" Ted says. "Aren't they great?"

I don't answer him for a moment. We're in the Yerba Buena Island tunnel halfway across the bridge. Ted curses and slows before a line of cars abreast at steady speed. He shoots across three lanes, finds an opening, and guns ahead. "Toadies," Mavis says. From my place in the jump seat the tunnel's yellowy white walls and intense lighting illumine her and Ted as if they are posed in a battery of floodlights. Then we're out of the tunnel. Fog is settling down over the city behind me. It gives the skyline the sheen of a glossy postcard. The sky ahead is clear, and

190   *Slides*

lights, mostly white, shine brightly along the East Bay. Off to the left of the bridge toward Berkeley the lights become greener, clustered like grapes on vines.

Ted glances at me over his shoulder. "Did you hear me? They're great, don't you think?"

I tell him they certainly are.

Then I say to Mavis, "That's some mother you've got."

"I'm marrying Mavis, not her mother," Ted says.

"Sure you are," I say.

Mavis leans into him, kisses his ear, and nibbles at it. "We'll love each other till the day we croak."

"Do you remember your father at all?" I say.

"Which one?"

"The real one."

Mavis turns and smiles at me. "No. Except from those stupid slides."

"What's this DeDe like?"

"You'd just love her." She describes some of DeDe's zany antics at parties. "Want me to call her, set something up?"

"I'll think about it," I say.

J'ACCUSE

I stand over his grave and read the tiny marker which will eventually be replaced by a large gray flat stone, financed by his accumulation of *pension invalide* funds at the Hôpital Psychiatrique where he has been a patient for the last 27 years:

```
        EMILE  PICKET

        1907 - 1997
```

The name is pronounced *Pee-kay*. Through the deep dirt barrier below I see his wizened brown stubbly face peering up at me quizzically as he used to from his hospital bed. I loved this strange little old man who represented for me a last bastion of cussedness, especially when it came to money.

He was not our first mad rebel, merely one in a long line, including some quite famous, thanks to the world-wide reputation of our founder, Dr. Oscar Forel. F. Scott Fitzgerald turned his wife, Zelda, over to Dr. Forel's care in the summer of 1930, long before my connection to the hospital began. Zelda stayed fifteen months until the fall of 1931. I have read letters between Scott and Zelda—they are touching and sad. Another patient that Dr. Forel diagnosed as a schizophrenic was James and Nora Joyce's daughter, Lucia. She stayed in Prangins in 1933 and 1934.

Les Rives de Prangins was designed for the well-to-do. It was like a country estate on a hundred acres of grounds, filled with blooming flowers and sculptured trees and bushes. The old sanitarium contained seven villas, four of which housed "guests": a duke here, a tycoon or an earl there, a Rothschild here, a Hohenzollern there. Now it's a cantonal hospital where medical insurance or *service social* pays for care. Most of our patients are psychotics or drunks.

Of the two, I've probably worked more with older alcoholics, until lately, when we began to take in SIDA victims. For them my heart twists in grief, especially for mothers and their infected babies, most of whom don't last long. My Swiss husband interprets the French version of AIDS as *Syndrome Imaginaire pour Décourager l'Amour*.

Why back then couldn't I make him my EX-husband?, I used to wonder. Whenever he made remarks like that, I wanted to cut out, yet for years I didn't. Why? Every time I entered the kitchen of our three-level condo in Nyon my shoulders would slump. Our meal together forced me to dwell on the pink granite of his face. And worse, to listen to him. I was able once, before we no longer touched, to put up with his cynicism, his callousness, his arrogance.

There's an old joke about Swiss men as lovers. Urs proved an exception at the beginning. We happened upon each other in Arizona's Petrified Forest while I was passing through on vacation from my nursing job in St. Louis. Urs, like so many Swiss, favors the American Southwest to visit because it's so different from his own country.

Even after I came to Switzerland we were all right for a few years. Then gradually I began to turn myself off, to shut down. Never quite enough, though. As he talked more, I found myself clenching my fists in my lap until the knuckles turned white.

When I'd put the dishes away and could retreat to my own floor, with my notebooks, my music, my drawings, my TV, I felt all right. I can put up with another day, I'd say to myself. I worked so hard to get that home—we both did. It surrounded us with so many elegant things that I sweat over to maintain. The prospect of giving them up made me almost sick. So I stayed. Yet . . . Monsieur Picket inspired me to vow that someday I'd declare myself: to hell with you, Urs, your things, your income, your outcome, your coldness, above all else, your coldness. Then, only then, would I be able to venture into the unknown.

Meantime I'd go back and forth to my shifts.

Oldtime co-workers tell me the hospital is different from when it held only the cultural elite. I don't know. Enter any asylum these days and you find variations on our own: a man who had sex with a cow then sliced it open and wrapped himself in its entrails; a woman who in her postpartum depression threw her baby out of a high window; a man trying constantly to remove the colonies of bees inhabiting his flesh up to his nostrils.

But M Picket was another story: utterly harmless in his paranoia. The police were always after him, or so he said. Spinning out a web of tales like Scheherezade, he claimed to have been arrested 1,001 times.

Because he was a favorite of Madame Squatt, the half-black chief of our service, he was allowed to keep a knife at his bedside (mostly for cutting apples, his favorite fruit). Possession of anything sharp is against the laws of the hospital, but he even had a pair of scissors, to accompany his sewing kit. He was an expert mender, tailor, leather worker.

He sat beside his bed, straight backed, little pot protruding into his pajama jacket. His fingers moved deftly as he repaired a strap from a purse belonging to Mme Squatt or sewed a tear in a jacket of mine or another nurse's. He sat the same way when he ran a brush through his white hair or trimmed his neat mustache. He took another position to polish the high boots that he always wore when he sneaked into town to have a drink. But in his last years he stopped going in, as he was becoming frail. After his blow-up over the money, he grew worse quickly.

He never wore glasses and swore that the cool water he splashed over his face every morning kept his vision intact. It may have aided his eyes, which were a bright blue, but by his 85th year he was nearly deaf. He heard when it mattered, though.

An illegitimate child born to a young Swiss peasant woman in a village near Lausanne, he began life twice bereft. He pricked his thumb as he told me about his begetters. Refusing my offer of a bandaid, he set his sewing on the bed beside him and sucked at the welling beads of blood. His father refused to recognize him, and his mother, in her grief and rage, hanged herself in a barn. The farm family that took him in worked him morning and night every day of the week save for one brief respite in church.

On a Sunday that began his 14th year, he feigned illness to stay home, then stole enough to run away. He twitched again in the telling, and his eyes grew moist.

He remained on the road the rest of his life, except for his years in institutions. Begging, cadging, scraping by, he worked his way around Europe. In those early times he never cared about money, let alone any savings—he was always broke and footloose. From the mid 1920s on, radicals attracted him to their causes. In 1937, he was arrested in Barcelona for conspiring to bomb a telephone exchange. Later he torched the offices of young fascists in Munich. The unoccupied home of a paint factory owner in postwar Copenhagen burnt to the ground after a nocturnal visit. M Picket's radicalism showed in his skull—he would lean his thinning mane forward to let me inspect the scars from three scrapes with police and strike breakers. In those years he supported himself by a thousand and one jobs, often housepainting.

His hero was Dreyfus, with whom he always identified as victim. Maybe too his first name made them compatriots, although I never learned whether he was named after Zola. Monsieur Picket's passion for Dreyfus had been so intense that after World War Two he made a special trip to the Montparnasse cemetery in Paris to pay homage to his hero. It pleased him to find Dreyfus buried with his entire family, but he confessed to me his bitter disappointment at discovering that Dreyfus had been elevated by the end of his military service to the rank of colonel. Monsieur Picket had no tolerance for high military ranks. Nevertheless, he saw himself when troubled, badgered, cornered as kinsman of Dreyfus and his own possible namesake, for then he would cry, "J'accuse . . .J'accuse . . . J'accuse."

As he grew older, his profits from his odd jobs increasingly went to drink. Try as he might, he could never accumulate any savings to tide him over. Our alcoholic wards are filled with vagabonds and housepainters. Maybe they need escape because they don't have any houses of their own to paint. In any case, drinking gave Monsieur Picket the nerve to go to Vevey to knock on the door of another of his heroes, Charlie Chaplin, who personally answered the door wearing white gloves. Drink also gave

M Picket the hatred to proclaim loudly in any working man's bar that the Pope was Satan Incarnate. Its excesses and absences led him in and out of three different institutions before Prangins.

In Prangins, he settled in. He had become, by then, an old codger, driven mad by his own demons and the chaotic century they had endured together. Yet often, more often than I ever thought possible, he was as rational as I. Having said so, I would next see him don a moth-eaten fez and a gaudy beaded brocade jacket, relics of his travels, and become a loony pasha lording over an empire in a vacant corner of his ward.

He stayed on the grounds except for those occasions when he felt the need to settle in at a sidewalk cafe in the village or in nearby Nyon for a night of quiet drinking. Then, with the aid of a driver, I would have to go rescue him. He never gave me any trouble, so long as I arrived late enough for him to be good and drunk. "Ah, l'Américaine," he would whisper, and tell me for the hundredth time that I was the only American he had ever known. But then he would also say, "You never confide in me the way Madame Squatt does. Why do you keep yourself so locked away?" I could not tell him my pain.

To solve these troublesome bouts of disappearance, Mme Squatt let him keep a bottle of Madeira in his closet. I envy the way she thumbs her nose at rules. Her father was a Libyan moor of dark cast; her mother Italian. Perhaps Mme Squatt identified with M Picket because she too had been abused as a child. Her affection for him was unusual because she didn't much care for men. Although we called her Madame, all of us knew that she had never married. Lucky soul.

Mme Squatt and I spoiled him in yet another way. He loved Turkish coffee. It's not easy to make. From finely ground coffee boiled up three times, we would serve him in his own special cup, the same cup he used for his wine. In its design nestled a red and white bird, of odd triangular shape. For his Turkish coffee, the cup was half-filled with sediment and heaped with sugar. He could take hours sipping it at a window overlooking Lake Geneva. He told me once that he loved the time when sun and sky combined to turn the lake into a giant silver platter.

If he liked me, he only liked me—he adored Mme Squatt. To reward her acts of kindness, he intended to leave her the bulk of his accumulated money, for he had in his late years finally become conscious of acquiring funds. But then the object of his planned largesse shifted. Here, I suppose it could be said, the troubles and the decline of Monsieur Picket began.

On one of his drinking soirées in Nyon, Monsieur Picket happened to sit at a table next to Dr. Armand Forel, who was holding forth on Swiss isolationism. This gentleman was a widely respected physician, humanist, and activist in the town for going on forty years. But he was also one of our more notorious citizens because of his stand as a militant communist in his early years.

Both Monsieur Picket and I were great admirers of the Forel family that went back into the 19th century in its line of distinguished doctors and scholars. Armand was the son of the late Dr. Oscar Forel, who had cared for both Zelda Fitzgerald and Lucia Joyce. Armand turned out to be very different from his father. For one thing, he had a private practice. For another, his every radical political view tended to stir up a hornet's nest among the Swiss. For many years he had served on the Grand Council as popiste deputy. As he grew older, Dr. Forel became increasingly critical of technocratic science and cybernetics. "Si nous continuons comme cela," he would cry, through his bristling gray mustache, "le monde court à la catastrophe."

That kind of talk was all Monsieur Picket needed to hear. Dazzled, he went into town as often as he was able, trying wherever he could to hear Dr. Forel speak. He became a follower partly for ideological reasons—"It is my last cause," he announced to me—but I believe that it was more Dr. Forel's fervor that enraptured the old man. Yet as Monsieur Picket grew more infirm, he had difficulty making it into town. He had by now pretty much decided to give Dr. Forel most of his savings.

When Dr. Forel's book, *Médecin et Homme Politique*, appeared, I said, "Why don't you buy copies of the book? He'd like that."

"No, I want him to have the money. He is our savior."

A savings mania overtook Monsieur Picket. He received five Swiss francs each weekday as pocket money; his invalid pension paid his hospital bill and also went into a modest pension fund. When saving for Mme Squatt, M Picket did not set aside all his weekly sum—he used some for his drinking excursions. But as he became carried away in his enthusiasm for Dr. Forel and more caught up by the force of the man's personality, he began to set aside a larger and larger percentage of his paltry allowance. So much so that he cut himself off entirely from drink and no longer even went into town. Intensely, he concentrated on building up his hoard. By putting away fifteen to twenty francs per week (say, $14), he was able to save about nine hundred francs in a year. After eight years of savings, he had the equivalent of six thousand American dollars. This money he had converted into large bills—seven 1,000 Swiss franc notes, to be exact. He would hold them clutched in one hand, his eyes glittering like a carrion bird's, even on those somewhat rare occasions when I would take his blood pressure.

"Why do you look that way?" he asked.

"You have sacrificed to save this money, you have denied yourself, you have suffered, and at the same time"—I had to smile—"you have improved your health. See, almost normal."

He looked up at me again. Color rose in his cheeks as he spoke of his love for Dr. Forel and Mme Squatt. They would soon have his money, five of the notes to Dr. Forel, two to Mme Squatt. He had no family of any sort, no children, no relatives, and only a few friends among the mad patients in the mixed ward where he lived. Not even they were entirely trustworthy. His eyes narrowed as he peered over his shoulder, on the watch for police ready to swoop down upon him at any moment. Then a sunny smile of his few remaining teeth broke through.

One day he spoke of his plans in the presence of one of the doctors, the same doctor who had twice misdiagnosed patients in my care. His cold eyes and superior manner reminded me of my husband's. Dr. Lupiné said to Monsieur Picket, "If you wish to leave money, you must arrange to do so through a lawyer. Remember, this money has come from your country to give you small pleasures."

"But I have denied these small pleasures to give money to the two people in the world that I love," said the old man, stricken.

"Nevertheless, you cannot do it without the necessary paper work," said the doctor, sniffing. "We have rules, you must abide by the rules."

The old man fumed, emitted an oath against the "police state," began to mutter, "J'accuse . . . J'accuse . . . ."

Over the next few days he asked me questions. I told him that I thought he could do what he wanted to do, since the money was his. But on his next rounds, Dr. Lupiné once again pestered him about seeking an attorney and filling out a series of forms.

"The attorney will direct you. You must complete paper work."

The old man retreated, muttering "J'accuse" again and again.

Although he had grown rickety, Monsieur Picket was still ambulatory. I watched him on a Wednesday walk out into the garden holding his money in his clenched fist. He also held his ceramic cup. From a window above, I saw him gather some sticks together, then some dry moss. At first I didn't know what he was doing. When I realized I raced down the stairs to try to stop him.

It was too late. He had already burnt the money. He had built a tiny funeral pyre, placed the cup in the center, and put the bills in. We both stood looking down at the charred wisps in the cup. I put my arm around his waist. It came to me then what I must do about my vows and all my lovely things. Was I mad enough? Monsieur Picket's eyes gave me my answer. To hell with you, pink granite husband. When only smoke came from the tinder he stooped to pick up the cup, and I led him shuffling back to his ward.

He sat in the same place for the next 36 hours, waiting for Dr. Lupiné to return. He would not let us budge him. Lord knows I tried, but he kept resisting fervently. His hands were formed around the cup in his lap as if he held a prized captive bird.

When the doctor appeared in the hallway, marching toward us like a Prussian officer, the old man painfully and slowly rose to his feet to block the path. I placed myself next to him to catch him, should he lose balance. His posture became erect without any help from me. He held his arms out, tipped the cup, and let the charred bits float to the floor.

"There . . . is your . . . paper work," the old man said.

Three weeks later, Monsieur Picket was dead.